The Gold Miner's Journal

THE ADVENTURES OF AN EARLY NEWS REPORTER

by
Branwen C. Patenaude

© Copyright 2004 Branwen C. Patenaude. All rights reserved.

No part of this publication may be reproduced, stored in a retrieval system, or transmitted, in any form or by any means, electronic, mechanical, photocopying, recording, or otherwise, without the written prior permission of the author. Printed in Victoria, BC, Canada

Note for Librarians: a cataloguing record for this book that includes Dewey Decimal Classification and US Library of Congress numbers is available from the National Library of Canada. The complete cataloguing record can be obtained from the National Library's online database at: www.nlc-bnc.ca/amicus/index-e.html
ISBN 1-4120-3664-X

TRAFFORD

Offices in Canada, USA, Ireland, UK and Spain
This book was published on-demand in cooperation with Trafford Publishing. On-demand publishing is a unique process and service of making a book available for retail sale to the public taking advantage of on-demand manufacturing and Internet marketing. On-demand publishing includes promotions, retail sales, manufacturing, order fulfilment, accounting and collecting royalties on behalf of the author.

Book sales in Europe:
Trafford Publishing (UK) Ltd., Enterprise House, Wistaston Road Business Centre, Wistaston Road, Crewe, Cheshire CW2 7RP UNITED KINGDOM
phone 01270 251 396 (local rate 0845 230 9601)
facsimile 01270 254 983; orders.uk@trafford.com

Book sales for North America and international:
Trafford Publishing, 6E–2333 Government St., Victoria, BC V8T 4P4 CANADA
phone 250 383 6864 (toll-free 1 888 232 4444)
fax 250 383 6804; email to orders@trafford.com

www.trafford.com/robots/04-1492.html

10 9 8 7 6 5 4 3 2

This novel is dedicated to my gold mining family;
my husband Wilfred H. Patenaude,
and our son David H. Patenaude

This referenced account is dedicated to all those brave pioneers who owned or worked as reporters on the *Cariboo Sentinel* newspaper, published in Barkerville, B.C. between 1865 and 1875

Contents

Chapter 1
The Boy from Newfoundland 11

Chapter 2
A Fearsome Journey 23

Chapter 3
Journey to Cottonwood 32

Chapter 4
A Winter of Experiences 49

Chapter 5
Road to the Goldfields 74

Chapter 6
A Rough Beginning in the Goldfields 84

Chapter 7
The Young Reporter 103

Chapter 8
The Missing Mine Owner 118

Chapter 9
The Miners of Antler Creek 145

Chapter 10
The Moving Corpse 173

Chapter 11
A Second Man Missing 187

Chapter 12
Of Ghouls and Gold Strikes 210

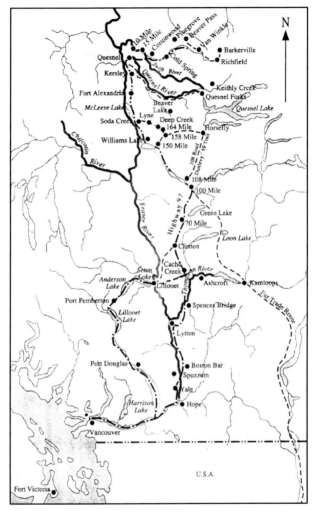

Map of Roads and Trails in British Columbia from 1858-2004

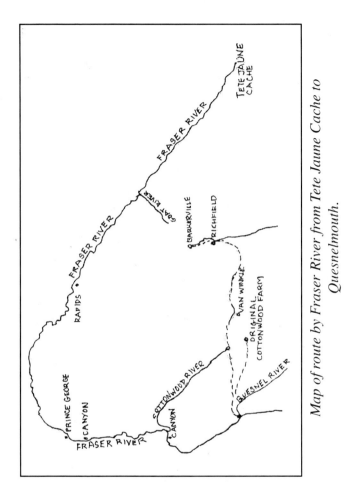

Map of route by Fraser River from Tete Jaune Cache to Quesnelmouth.

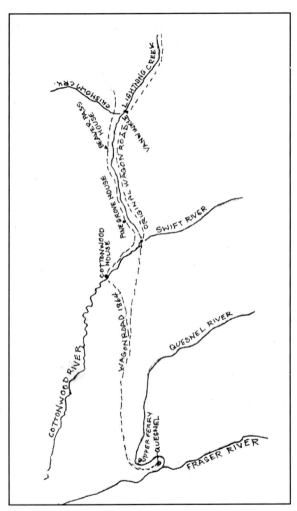

Map of original trail and wagon route from Quesnelmouth to Williams Creek

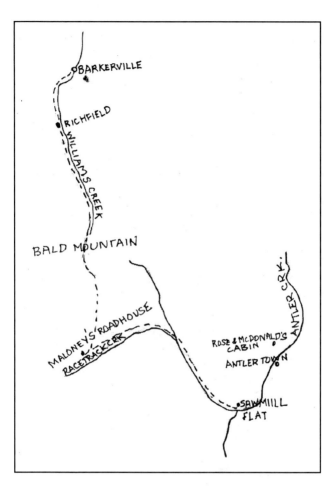

Map of route from Williams Creek to Antler Creek.

CHAPTER 1

The Boy from Newfoundland

As Dan mingled with the crowd leaving the Richfield courthouse that sunny, summer afternoon, he saw Henry Felker emerging from a side door with the policeman, and his lawyer, Mr. Walker. Half running through the throng of curious onlookers he reached Felker.

"Could I have your comments on the inquiry Sir? Do you think it was fair? No doubt your family will miss you while you are in jail, waiting for Judge Begbie" said Dan, all in one breath.

Felker took a step back, put up his fists, and would have knocked the young reporter down had not Mr. Walker held him back.

"Got in Himmel", Felker swore in his strong German accent, "Can't you leave a man alone?" Undaunted Dan sprang forward again,

"Sorry Sir, I was only trying to get a story for the press, Sir". Realizing his intrusion would yield him nothing more in the way of news, Dan retreated to watch, as the three men walked slowly down the hill to the police station. He wondered how a man like Felker could have got into such a scrape.

A hard working German immigrant, Henry Felker and his family of numerous children had settled in the Cariboo on a preemption just north of Lac La Hache, in

1862, where they operated a cattle ranch and dairy, and grew a large vegetable garden.

During the summer months Henry quite regularly transported milk, cream, cheese, and vegetables by horse and wagon to the gold rush town on Williams Creek, a distance of over a hundred miles north.

While it was hard work, the ranch and dairy did provide a living for his wife and seven young children; but Henry's heart was not in farming; for he was miner, and had gold fever.

After many quarrels he had agreed to preempt the land to appease his wife Antonette, who had spent many years traipsing around after Henry where he had mined in California, and more recently on the lower Fraser River near Yale.

Once settled on a farm in the Cariboo Antonette declared that she would never move again.

Henry, on the other hand, had not given up his craving for the mining game, in other words, he still had 'gold fever'. Secretly he told himself:

'On my next trip to the gold fields I am going to go to the mining office to see about staking a claim.

This ranching business takes up all my time, and does not interest me.'

Although of a gregarious nature, Henry was not given to serious drinking. On this occasion however, having sold his vegetables and dairy products, he had stopped for a drink in a local saloon before starting for home.

Sitting at the same table with him was a man named

Bibel, who was also from Germany.

Henry enjoyed conversing with the man in his native tongue, although there were others at the same table who objected.

"Hey you Krouts, here in Canada we speak English." they called out, but to which Henry and his companion paid no attention.

As the evening wore on, the two men kept on drinking and began to disagree on various matters, and to fight.

At this point reason did prevail when Felker decided that it was time to leave, and rose from his seat. Just as Henry was about to reach the door, Bibel attacked Felker with a sharp object, described later as an ice pick A moment before the blow hit him, Felker put out his foot and tripped Bibel, who fell on his head.

Taken to the local hospital on Williams Creek, Bibel lingered in and out of consciousness for two weeks, before he died.

Not long after this a policeman arrived at the Felker ranch to arrest Henry. He was charged with murder, and taken back to Richfield, where he was incarcerated for several months before coming before Judge Begbie at the Fall Assizes.

Walking back into town, Dan McDermott entered the office of the Cariboo Sentinel newspaper where it was located, across the street from the fire hall and the Theatre Royal.

"Well, did you speak with Felker?" asked George

Wallace the Editor.

"Pretty upset, he was" replied Dan, "nearly knocked me down when I tried to get an interview; but I do have some notes from the court proceedings."

"If you are going to be a good reporter you can expect to suffer all sorts of indignities" advised George as he stood beside the 'chase' he was assembling, "Anyway, now that you are back, you can compose your notes, and then help me get this paper out."

The Cariboo Sentinel, a weekly, four page newspaper published in Barkerville, supplied its readers with the latest news of the various, rich placer gold mines in the area, as well as the comings and goings of its residents. When something as sensational as a murder occurred, the paper was full of it.

Daniel McDermott the reporter for the 'Sentinel', was a tall, good looking, freckle faced boy of fifteen when he first reached Williams Creek

He had grown up on the coast of Newfoundland, in the small community of Carbonear, where he was the eldest in a family of eight children.

As were most of the population there, his father was a fisherman, and Dan, at an early age, was taken out to sea to learn the business, which he grew to hate.

He might not have found it so intolerable if his father had shown him more patience. At such an early age Dan was just not strong enough to handle the large heavy net, and when he unfortunately reeled it in backwards one day, causing all the fish to escape, his father beat him, almost senseless. After that he had refused to go fishing.

Although he had attended school for a few years, most of Dan's knowledge of the world came from books he had borrowed from a local school teacher.

Reading became a passion, and he found himself spending more and more time in his bedroom, absorbed in a wide spectrum of material from which he wrote short stories, some from his own imagination.

'Some day,' he told himself 'I think I could write for a living.'

"Where is that boy?" he could hear his father storming around down stairs, complaining to his mother,

"How will he ever learn to make a living when he sits reading in his room all day?"

As he grew older Dan yearned for excitement, and the opportunity to see some of the world that he had read about.

When news of the gold rush in far off British Columbia reached him, it set him to dreaming of a whole new world where he might find adventure, and even a fortune, if he could only get there.

As he packed some clothes and toiletries, he went to a drawer in his dresser where he kept a locked box. From this he took out a $10. gold piece that had been a gift from his grandfather when he was christened, and placed it in a secret pocket in his knap sack

'It should be safe there' he said to himself.

It was late one night in March when he left home, his bed roll and knap sack on his back.

Dan leaves home.

As he stole out of the house he didn't even stop to say goodbye. He knew his mother would cry if she knew he was leaving, and there would be a scene.

It was much better this way.

In touch with friends, Dan had been told that several groups of men from Upper Canada were leaving that spring for the west, and were in fact heading for the Cariboo gold fields in British Columbia. If he hurried he could catch up with one group in St. Paul, Minnesota, from where they would travel west. It was expected that they would reach the gold fields by mid summer.

In actual fact Dan did not reach the Cariboo for another two years.

Travelling for the first several months with a group of men of the McMicking party of 'Overlanders', as they came to be known, they arrived at Fort Garry, a Hudson's Bay Company fort, about half way across the country.

It was here that Dan decided he would not continue with the group. He had had a falling out with the leader, who accused him of sponging off the other men, and not pulling his weight. It was true that he had no money, but Dan had worked hard, and always volunteered whenever help was needed. Receiving no encouragement to continue on with the group, he remained behind.

During the winter at Fort Garry he managed to find work in a flour mill outside the fort, where he boarded with the owners, a Scottish family, until spring came and he could travel again.

The owners of the mill, Mr. and Mrs. Robert McTavish, were third generation Scots in Canada, and Mr. McTavish had inherited the mill from his father before him. It was through their son Jamie, the same age as Dan, that Dan found work.

Having abandoned the 'Overlander' group, Dan was tramping along outside Fort Garry, wondering what to do next, when an enormous dog, a Great Dane, came bounding along the trail toward him. When the dog spotted Dan, it began to bark. Close behind was Jamie Mctavish, the owner. As the dog closed in on him, Dan backed away, afraid of the dog's deep growls, and vicious sounding snarls.

"Here Rex", called Jamie several times before the dog ran back to him. Grabbing the dog's collar, he held the dog at bay.

"He won't bite you", called Jamie, he just sounds vicious.

"You could have fooled me" replied Dan, "I am not used to dogs.

This caused a conversation between the boys, and the start of a friendship.

Discovering that Dan was alone and without a place to stay, Jamie invited him to his home near the mill.

"I could use you in the mill for the winter" offered Bob McTavish, but I can't pay you much."

"Whatever you can afford, Sir, I would be grateful for even a roof over my head."

Dan and Jamie became good friends over the winter, and except for Dan's discouragement, Jamie might

18

have left home with Dan when spring came.

"You have loving parents, Jamie, and a bright future here" he told him, "my future is most uncertain."

By April of the next year Dan had joined another group of 'Overlanders' who were also headed west for the gold fields of the Cariboo. That summer they reached Tete Juan Cache, a jumping off place on the upper Fraser River, close to the borders of British Columbia and Rupert's Land.

While the men of the group were busy deciding how they would proceed from there, whether it be overland, or on rafts down the Fraser River, Dan noticed another small group of men who were busy building a barge of Cottonwood trees. They were using strips of green bark to bind the logs together.

'These men are preparing to travel down the river' Dan said to himself as he wandered over to them.

"Don't you have any rope?" he inquired of a tall, middle aged man. The man looked up from his work, while two others ignored him and kept on working.

"If we did we would be using it", was the reply.

"Are you going down the river?" Dan asked. The man looked up again.

"Just as soon as we are ready" he answered.

"How far are you going?" asked Dan once more.

"As far as Quesnelmouth, if we are lucky" the man replied.

Just then another man of the group, a dark haired man with a strong Welsh accent whispered to the first man,

"Ask him if he wants to go with us." At that a third man spoke up.

"We are merchants from near Fort Garry, and we are going down the Fraser River with our goods to open a store at Quesnelmouth"

"Would you take me along with you?" asked Dan. The thought of travelling by water appealed to him, for he had sailed the Atlantic in fish boats for most of his life.

"If we took you, would you be willing to work on the barge, make meals, use the oars when we need them, and keep watch at night?" asked the tall man?"

"Indeed I would" agreed Dan, who proceeded to tell them of his own experiences on boats while growing up on the Atlantic coast.

There were many preparations to be made before they could leave on the journey.

The barge they were building was about fourteen feet wide, and thirty feet long. Dan was put to work helping one of the men cut strips of bark from the trees.

"Here young fella, take this knife, and watch me. Be careful though, we don't want you to cut yourself before the journey even begins" commented the tall man, whose name was Tom

That night, around a campfire Dan met the other three men, Joe, and Owen, two Welsh partners, and Felix, a Jewish merchant, who was Tom's partner.

None of these men had operated a barge on a river

before, much less on the Fraser River which was beset with dangerous rapids and whirlpools.

As supplies were brought to the barge site an oxen was killed, and two native women were hired to cut it up and dry and jerk the meat, so that it would keep during the journey. Dan watched the women skinning the carcass. They were very adept at the task, using sharp stones, rather than knives, to work with. It was not long before the hide was free from the meat and stretched over a wooden frame to dry.

From the local natives the merchants bought pemmican, sewn up in animal bladders. Dan had not seen anything like these before.

"Let me look inside the bag" he asked an Indian woman as he took hold of one. The woman grabbed it back, shaking her head in a most negative manner.

"No no" called Joe, one of the merchants, "don't open it, the bags of pemmican are sealed and should not be opened until they are used"

"What is pemmican?" asked Dan.

"It is good food on a journey. Dried berries and cooked meat, sealed in fat." explained Felix, the eldest of the merchants.

There was also some bartering done over a number of large salmon wrapped in wet, green leaves which, they were instructed, should either be smoked and dried, or eaten before the flies got on them.

The natives had been eyeing some blankets that were among the merchant's goods, and so an exchange was made, one wool blanket for every dozen large salmon.

The merchants' saleable goods were piled up and fastened down in the middle of the raft, with waterproof tarpaulins spread over them. To Dan it looked like an expensive cargo to transport down river on a barge, but obviously a much cheaper way than taking it overland.

Finally on September 20, on a late, rainy afternoon, they were ready to leave. As the four men and Dan boarded the barge and pushed off the beach with their oars, a collection of native men and women stood silently by, watching their departure.

As they stood there they passed many comments between them.

"Think they'll make it to Quesnelemouth?" asked one.

"Pretty treacherous for green horns, especially through those rapids." ventured another, as the raft disappeared around the first bend.

CHAPTER 2

The Fearsome Journey

The river for some distance downstream from the Cache was very crooked, with a strong current, and in some places, was very narrow. With sheer rock cliffs on both sides, and hidden rocks in the shallows, it was difficult to keep the barge afloat.

"Get that stove going, boy, and make us some strong coffee", yelled Tom as Dan put down his oar. Just behind the cargo, in the most sheltered spot on the barge, was a small cook stove, and close to it, a sack of charcoal. Dan boiled a pot of water and then searched through the groceries under the tarpaulin, until he found a can of Hudson's Bay Moca Java coffee, and a tin cup. From this he metered out a quantity of the dark brown grains into the boiling water.

'At least these men are Canadians' said Dan to himself, 'although they have probably been to the California goldrush'. Felix, the eldest of the four was a German Jew. Dan realized this when evening came and Felix rolled out his little prayer mat, kneeled, and chanted in Hebrew.

When the two Welshmen, Owen and Tom came to drink some of Dan's coffee, they praised him, "Good brew young fella" remarked Tom, as he drew a flask of rum from his breast pocket and added it to his coffee.

23

Owen, a brawny young man, the younger of the two Welshmen, was also about to praise Dan, and started to put his arm around Dan, but Dan quickly moved away.

'Strange behavior for a man who has just met me.' thought Dan.

"I can see you are going to fit in just fine, young fella" purred Owen.

Suddenly a thought came to Dan, 'Perhaps Owen is gay.' He had read about such people, women also, who were attracted to others of the same sex. Growing up in a large family of boys and girls, the subject of sex had never occurred to him; and he had been too young to have a girlfriend. The thought of having sexual relations with a man repulsed him.

As daylight fell that first day, they steered the barge into a sheltered bay for the night. It was estimated they had gone about seventy miles.

The next morning as they rose from their blankets it was not yet daylight, and a stiff breeze was blowing a steady drizzle of rain.

They could see that the river downstream was slowing its pace as it ran through a wide valley of fairly flat, heavily timbered land. The further they went, the more slowly the river ran, until they finally reached a point where they were hardly moving at all. They had not yet had breakfast when Joe shouted to them:

"Get on those oars, and row hard, boys. We're never going to get anywhere this way." Dan had just put his oar in the water when Owen came along side of him.

"That Joe, he thinks he can boss us all. We are

doing just fine; what's the big rush anyway?" he complained.

"He wants to get down the river as fast as possible, before winter comes" suggested Dan.

"He'll change his tune when we reach those rapids," commented Owen, "and I'm not looking forward to that." By the fourth day the rain had stopped, and the sun came out from behind the clouds. As Dan sat resting on a pile of tarps, enjoying the warmth of the sun, he almost went to sleep. The unusual exertion of rowing, and learning to keep his balance on the continually moving barge, had his body aching all over. His hands perhaps, were suffering the most. Covered with blisters that had burst, he had had to wrap them in cloths. They stung terribly. But for now he was enjoying the excitement of watching the changing mood of the river, and anticipating the dreaded rapids that were expected to appear at any time.

Sure enough, by the next day the muddy coloured river had narrowed, and was running faster by the minute.

Looking downstream for about a quarter of a mile, all that could be seen was white foam rising from a turbulent mass of water. It was a big rapids!

Instead of sailing straight into them they found a quiet bay, into which they pulled the barge.

"Tom and Felix and I will walk downstream to examine the extent of the rapids" Joe, told Owen and Dan.

While they were gone Dan busied himself with

tightening the ropes on the tarps, and generally making sure everything was secure in readiness for the ride through the rapids. Only Owen and Dan had remained on board.

Up until now Dan had not had much to do with Owen, and in fact had avoided him as much as possible. There was something about Owen that made Dan's skin crawl.

'I think we have a homosexual amongst us' he told himself. He had been going to mention this to Joe, to see what he had to say about Owen, but the right moment had never come along. Now with all the other men gone, Dan noticed Owen approaching him where he worked in the middle of the barge.

Not wanting to encounter him Dan moved down to the other end. He quickly realized he had made a mistake, he should have remained by the cargo, where he had more room to escape, if necessary.

But it was too late to move again. There at the far end of the barge he was cornered. Owen came toward him, and when he got close enough, he seized Dan by the waist while Dan struggled to get away.

"Come here you delicious young thing. Do you know how I have wanted you, right from the day I first saw you?"

The more Dan struggled, the tighter Owen held him, and slowly he pushed Dan down on to the floor of the barge, all the while rubbing him on his private parts, and humming in his ear. Still struggling, Dan was desperate, and tried to move himself closer to the edge of the barge. If he could push Owen into the river, he could probably break free of him. Just as Owen was about to tear off Dan's britches, they both heard and felt a great weight landing on the barge.

'Thank goodness' thought Dan, 'someone has arrived back! As Owen quickly released Dan, and as they both rose from the deck and looked up, they could see it was not one of the men arriving back, but a large cougar, that had probably smelled food, and had jumped onboard the barge to investigate.

Recovering themselves, both Owen and Dan crept forward to where several rifles were stored under the tarpaulines. The cougar, a large male, was headed their way, toward the food supply, but before the creature could reach it, Owen managed to put his hands on a loaded shotgun, and fired. The bullet missed the cougar, that instantly ran past them, jumped off the barge, and disappeared into the trees above the beach. Meanwhile Dan had also seized the opportunity to jump off the barge, and quickly ran up the beach, and into the trees.

A large, male cougar jumped aboard the raft.

Unconcerned about the cougar, his fear was that Owen would fire at him too, so he kept himself hidden. Fortunately Owen did not seek him out.

It was another half an hour before Joe and Felix came back, with Tom following behind. They had heard the shot, and thought there might be trouble.

When the other men returned, Dan walked out of the woods and jumped back on to the barge, but because the men were so concerned about the cougar, he did not get a chance to complain about Owen.

The investigation downstream had revealed that the rapids consisted of three distinct stretches, each one at least a quarter of a mile long.

They also discovered that it was possible to portage around two of the rapids. With this in mind, they unloaded as much of the valuable cargo as could be carried, and while Tom, who could not swim, and Felix, made two trips with the cargo, Joe, Owen, and Dan, took the barge down through the first two sets of rapids.

Once into the current of the river, the fast flowing stream swept the barge out into the swirling, surging white water. On their right was a rocky reef against which the boiling mass was lashing itself into a wall of foam, threatening them with instant destruction. On the other was a seething and eddying whirlpool, ready to engulf any mortal who might come within its reach.

As the men steered the barge right through the middle of the formidable mass, total destruction seemed inevitable.

No one dared speak a word except the pilot, Joe, who issued orders to the others.

"Row like hell on the right", and "turn your left NOW", and at one point, he was himself nearly swept overboard

Almost through the worst of the rapids, the barge suddenly shot too close to a sharp rock, which tore away a ten foot log from one side, before it glided safely down into a quiet pool below.

By the time they reached the third and most dangerous set of rapids, the five men were working like a team and seemed less afraid of the terrible dangers.

Although they knew they still stood the chance of overturning the barge, drowning, and losing everything, they fortunately came through the ordeal without any further mishap.

At Fort George they rested for two days, where Tom and Felix met the Hudson's Bay Factor Thomas Charles, and where they all helped to repair the barge.

It had been a bright, sunny, fall day when they arrived, but by the next day it had grown colder with an overcast sky, and by noon the first heavy snow storm of the winter swept through the area, leaving two inches of snow upon the ground.

From the Factor they learned of even more dangerous canyons downstream from Fort George, one fifteen miles below, and the other, the Cottonwood Canyon, a few miles north of the mouth of the Quesnelle River.

Talking it over, the men determined it would be wise to hire a guide to direct them through the worst of the rapids, if one could be found.

Before leaving on their journey downstream, they purchased fresh vegetables, and root crops, which they dug from the Hudson's Bay Co. garden.

By now they had eaten what they could of their fresh meat and fish on the barge, before it became fly blown, but were able to replace it with bear, beaver and badger meat, bought from the Indians.

A native guide accompanied them down river with the barge, and guided them through the two sets of fearsome rapids.

The most terrifying part of the Fort George Canyon was a 'shelving' rock out in the middle of the main channel, through which a large body of water boiled for some distance, then fell off and formed a double whirlpool below.

On orders from the guide, they moved the raft from one side of the main mass to the other, and with all four men rowing as hard as they could, they came out of it intact, and slid into another quiet pool at the other end.

Immediately below the rapids they passed by a company of Chinese miners, the first of many small parties working the river bars for about ten miles, all the way to the little community of Quesnelle.

It was after dark when they arrived and moored the barge close to the steamer dock just upstream from the mouth of the Quesnelle River.

Due to the lateness of the hour, they all retired until morning, all except the native guide, who left to stay with relatives at the local reserve nearby.

CHAPTER 3

Journey to Cottonwood

The next morning found Dan helping the merchants to unload their goods from the barge and into a warehouse some fifty feet up the bank. With this done, Dan bid his companions farewell.

"You are a good worker, Dan," said Joe as they all shook hands, "you will succeed, I'm sure, in whatever you choose to do. Before you go though, I want to give you $10 in cash, and something else that might be useful on your journey to the gold fields".

With that Felix brought forth a brand new rifle, and a box of shells. Dan was both pleased and surprised, for he had not counted on such generosity. Thanking them profusely, he put the money away into his jacket pocket, and tucked the gun under his arm. As he walked away, he thought to himself

'I never did have a chance to talk to Tom about Owen.' Of course nothing more had happened since that one encounter, and Dan made sure he kept his distance from the unsavory Welshman.

By this time it was midday, and not having had anything to eat that day, he went looking for the possibility of a meal.

Not far from where he had helped to unload the barge, he had noticed a group of men seated around a campfire. From the tantalizing smell that wafted across the beach, it was obvious to Dan that someone was cooking sausages.

Sure enough it was a miner, a Mr. Whitehall, who, although he was without a building, had made a fire and was feeding customers from a rough hewn, wooden table.

"Hello there, Sir", called Dan, "I've just arrived down the river from Tete Juan Cache and if you will feed me, I will do almost any manner of work to pay for it." Although he did now have some money, he was not going to part with any of it, if he could help it." Jake Whitehall, who recognized Dan's young age, was agreeable.

"Take this axe and cut down some dead branches for my camp fire. I need some right away, so get me an armful quickly, and I'll have your meal ready."

This was easy work, for the forest was just behind them, a dense forest of large fir and spruce trees, and amongst them, he could see a number of dead snags. As Dan returned with the firewood, Whitehall motioned him to a stump and handed him a tin plate of sausages and beans, a few slices of sourdough bread, and a cup of hot coffee.

As he sat there enjoying the food, he noticed two other men sitting close by, who were also having a meal. Turning toward them Dan asked,

"Can you tell me how to get on the trail to the gold fields?" The men looked at each other, and after a moment or two the older man, who had his hat pulled down almost over his eyes, replied.

"Did you run away from school lad? Your Ma will be missing you." then they both burst out laughing. Dan ignored them, and approached

Mr. Whitehall who had heard the conversation.

"Don't take any notice of those men, follow the trail up the Quesnel River for about four miles, lad, until you come to Henry Cock's roadhouse farm at Four Mile Creek. Once you get there, you can ask for further directions."

As he finished eating his meal, Dan worked for another hour to supply Mr. Whitehall with a stack of dry wood before he headed east, beside the Quesnelle River.

Along the way, Dan thought about the men back at the fire who had laughed at him.

'Did he look that young?' he asked himself. 'What's wrong with being young? As long as I am able to take care of myself, I'll make out. After all, he had come this far!' he reassured himself. Just then he stubbed his toe on a rock and fell headlong into a bush of stinging nettles.

'Ouch, ouch', he cried, as he stood up again. During the fall, his shoe had come off, and as he put it back on, he noticed the large holes in the soles of both shoes.

'Well, it's no wonder', he thought, 'considering all the miles I have walked!'

His clothes too, were showing definite signs of wear, and his socks had been turned so many times

34

there was hardly a place without a hole.

The path through the woods ran parallel to the Quesnelle River, and as he walked along he admired the clear turquoise colour of the swiftly flowing water that had traveled all the way from the glaciers, to meet the muddy Fraser River.

By the river's edge were little Water Woozles, small birds with long thin beaks, who were darting in and out of the stream, fluttering their feathers and diving for insects and other edible matter.

After some time, and as Dan rounded a corner of the trail and looked upstream, he could see a fenced meadow beside the river, where several horses and cows were pastured. Over on the opposite bank of the river a rope ferry was plying its way across. On board were three men, and following close behind were their mules, snorting and blowing as they swam, their long ears visible above the water.

Still farther on, built against the heavily forested hillside, was a large log cabin with a shake roof. A column of grey smoke rose from the two stone and grass chimneys, built on either end of the cabin.

'This must be Henry Cock's Four Mile ferry and farm ' thought Dan.

Approaching the cabin through a field of recently cut hay, Dan could hear voices, a deep male voice, and the high pitched shrill of a female.

On entering the door he encountered a man standing with his arm around the waist of a handsome, middle-aged woman.

"Stand away from me, John, you big oaf", cried the woman", or I'll clobber you with my heavy frying pan".

On seeing Dan, John loosened his hold on the woman, stepped back, and sat down on a bench alongside the long, home made table. After making himself known Dan asked the woman,

"Have you some hot coffee on hand? I have worked up quite a thirst on my walk from the river's mouth, and it is growing cold out there, with a sharp wind blowing up the river."

"Indeed I have", smiled the woman, amused at Dan's eloquent speech and his Newfoundland accent.

"I also have some beef stew if you are wanting some." she said as she stoked up the fire in her large cast iron cook stove."

"Oooh," exclaimed Dan, "that sounds good, I have not tasted beef for some time;

"50cts for you, gossoon." the woman crooned.

As his eyes adjusted to the dimly lit room Dan's attention was drawn to the small, single window facing the river, and to four other men seated beside a fireplace in the back corner of the room.

"Where are you headed, young fella?" inquired one of the men.

"I am heading for Williams Creek", called Dan.

"Too late to dig for gold this year." replied the man.

"Yes, I know", called Dan, "but I will find somewhere along the way to earn my keep until spring".

"You could try the farm at Cottonwood", suggested one man. "That's about twenty five miles east of here".

"You can bed down here for the night, if you want to", offered the Irish housekeeper, "I'll only charge you twenty five cents, and another twenty five for your breakfast tomorrow."

"Thanks", said Dan, "but I'd best be on my way, I can still put in a few miles before dark"

As he left the cabin and began to climb the steep hill behind, he realized he would probably be spending the night alone, under a tree.

'Let me see,' he said to himself as he thought about what food he had left in his knap sack.

As he opened the pack, and rummaged through it, he found part of a loaf of bread, a little coffee, and a partly eaten ham bone.

'So I'll not starve.' he thought.

On reaching the summit of the hill Dan encountered a second trail coming in from the east that appeared to be going in the direction of Williams Creek. This trail was wider, and beaten down with the tracks of many cattle having passed over it very recently. The animals had left many piles of dung, which gave off an offensive smell.

Hurrying on, and walking on the far outside of the trail, Dan came across a group of three European men, and just in front of them, were two Chinese. The Orientals, dressed in their loose, baggy pants and buttoned up shirts, were minding their own business, hurrying toward Quesnelle

The white men were harassing the Chinese, hurling verbal insults, and throwing stones at them.

"Why do you treat the Chinese so cruelly?" Dan asked.

"Because they do not fight back", giggled one man,

"They smell funny", said another.

"Let them be", called Dan, "they aren't harming you, and besides that, when was the last time you took a bath?" At that the three men surrounded Dan and began to taunt him.

"Chinky Chinky Chinaman", they chanted.

The Chinese understood enough English to realize that while Dan was defending them, he too was being harassed. With this they stopped and turned on their tormentors. One of the Chinese produced a cleaver, and the other, a long butcher knife. This took the men by surprise, and sent them scurrying for the bush. Once they were gone the Chinese men shook Dan's hand, bowed low, and continued on their way.

As he hiked along, Dan noticed that the smell of cattle and their leavings was not diminishing, and in fact was getting stronger.

From a clearing where he could see the trail ahead, a big cloud of dust told him that he was catching up to the cattle. Drawing closer he could hear the cattle bawling, and men shouting and whistling.

Within another mile he had caught up with several cowboys pushing a large herd of cattle along the trail. Diving into the woods Dan managed to find his way through the timber, from where he watched the procession. When one of the men dismounted to relieve himself Dan approached him. The man was surprised to see him

"Where did you come from? I did not notice you on the trail", he mentioned as he pulled out his tobacco pouch and began to roll a cigarette.

"Where are you taking these cattle?" Dan asked.

"As far as the Cottonwood ranch, where they will be pastured until they are butchered and sold to the mining camps." the man replied

"How far are we from there?" Dan asked again.

"Hmm, we should be there by dark" replied the cowboy as he lit up.

"Need any help?" Dan asked again.

"Well, if you want to walk on for about another mile, you could make a fire somewhere beside the road. We sure could use a swallow of coffee to cut down the dust in our throats. You will find the makings on my horse there."

Dan signaled his willingness and walked over to the horse where he found a bag of supplies tied to the saddle.

Almost an hour later Dan had a hot fire burning in a small clearing beside the trail, and a brew of strong coffee waiting in a large tin can.

While Dan waited for the cowboys to come for coffee, he thought about the $10. gold piece he had in his jacket, the one that Joe, the merchant had given him.

'I shouldn't leave it in my jacket. I will put it in my secret pocket' he said to himself, 'along with the one grandpa gave me.'

As he dug around in the pocket, he realized that the original gold piece, the one he had been given at his christening, was gone. 'What could have happened to it' he wondered, 'Did someone steal it?

One by one the several cowboys rode up to the fire and helped themselves to the coffee. They seemed grateful for the break

"We have been on this drive for nearly a month now", volunteered one young drover.

"Where did you start from?" Dan asked the owner of the herd.

"This spring my partner here," and he nudged a man standing beside him, "started from Hat Creek on the Bonaparte River. Actually though, it has been over a year since we left home in Oregon. When we realized we were too late to reach market last fall, we wintered over at Hat Creek where there was good feed for the cattle."

"So it has taken you several weeks to get this far?" commented Dan

"Well, we were held up at Quesnelmouth for several days. The forest there is so dense that several cattle strayed away from the herd. It took us all that time to find them, and round them up."

As the last of the cowboys finished his coffee Dan put out the fire, washed the pot and the cups in a nearby creek, and returned the supplies to the head cattleman, Jerome Harper.

"We thank you for your help" shouted the American above the lowing of cattle and hollering of his men.

"You saved us a lot of time and trouble." echoed his partner Ned Tormey who had got off his horse to talk to Dan

"You are a willing worker and make a good cup of coffee. For that we would like you to accept this" and he pressed something heavy into Dan's hand. On looking down at the shiny orb he recognized an American silver dollar.

As Dan watched the riders and their charges disappear up the trail he once again took a path through the woods to get ahead of the noisy, worrisome, cattle.

Here it was cool and quiet, where the Jay birds and the Chicadees called, and the squirrels flitted from tree to tree, gathering pine cones for the coming winter.

Back on the trail, and a few miles further on, evening shadows were falling across his path.

Dan knew he was getting very weary when he began to stumble over the stones on the rough trail.

Watching for an accommodating tree to get under for the night, the trail suddenly ended, down hill to the banks of a fairly large, but quiet flowing river. On the other side he could see a cluster of log buildings, and from a window came the glimmer of a light.

With habitation so close by, Dan decided he would

go a bit further.

'But how to get across the river? Surely he wouldn't have to swim' Dan wondered. Then in the shadow of the riverbank he noticed a rowboat moored on the opposite bank.

'It's a ferry' he said to himself, and with that he began to call in a loud voice.

"Mr. ferryman, are you there? I need a ride. If you are there, please answer. I can pay you to come across for me."

It seemed like an eternity before his calls were answered, but finally a man came out of a small shack in the trees, and climbed down the bank to the boat.

"I'm coming, I'm coming", the man called back in a grumpy tone of voice. "You can stop your hollering now, before you wake the dead. I wasn't expecting any more traffic tonight."

A few minutes later the boat arrived across the quiet stream, driven by an elderly native man with a shock of white hair. As Dan climbed in, the man looked up at Dan and mentioned,

"You're a very young wipper snapper to be so far from home, aren't you ?"

"Well, I've made it this far, all the way from Newfoundland I have" boasted Dan.

"Going to the gold fields, are you? asked the man.

"Yes, I know I'm too late for this year", replied Dan before the ferryman could mention it, "but I thought I'd winter over somewhere."

"Try here at this ranch, they could probably use

a young fella like you." said the ferryman as the boat landed on the east bank.

"Here's 20cts", is that enough for the ride?" asked Dan.

"Yes, that'll do, I usually charge 50cts. but for you, 20cts. will do" muttered the man.

As Dan trudged wearily up the trail toward the buildings and the one light he had seen, he passed by open, grassy pastures and large log corrals, all of which were devoid of life.

He noticed that the gate into the largest corral was open, as if the owners were expecting to use it soon.

Dan found his way to what looked like the front door of the main house. It was a large, sturdy looking, single story log building with very few windows. Dan had been told that this was typical of most houses in the Cariboo, where the winters were long and often very cold.

Knocking loudly on the heavy, wooden, front door, it was a few minutes before anyone came. Finally, just as Dan was about to knock again, the door opened, and a short stocky man in his late forties greeted him. Dan noticed his greying hair and the large red scar on his right cheek.

"Hello there young man, it's rather late for one so young to be out, but what can I do for you?"

"Well sir, I've come all the way from Newfoundland to reach the goldfields. I know I'm too late for this year, but I can't go home, and I'm looking for somewhere to stay over the winter.

I will work hard for my board, if I can just stay. until spring. By the way, there's a large herd of cattle headed your way, I met them on the trail about half an hour ago. Can I stay here?"

"You look very young, but if you are willing to work hard I think we could keep you. So you ran away from home did you? Yes we've had quite a few of those this year, everyone is going to the gold rush." replied the man

"Are you in charge here Sir?" asked Dan.

"Yes, replied the man, "I am Charles Heath, co-owner of this Cottonwood ranch.

"Who is the other owner?" Dan asked

"John Boyd, he is my partner, but anyway, I'm sure you are tired from your long walk, and probably hungry too. Come this way, and we'll see what we can find. Dinner is usually at about 5.00 o'clock around here, but the cook might still be up."

Heath led Dan to the rear of the house where there was a kitchen, a large room containing a big cast iron cook stove with double ovens and warming ovens. An open fireplace faced with mortared rocks was burning at the far end of the room, and beside it was a big round wooden table.

Here sat a rather corpulent Chinese man, fast asleep. His flabby body encased in a long, black, cotton gown, was slumped over the table. His head, with a growth of long, thick, black hair, braided up at the back in a pigtail, lay on the table, with his arms and hands hidden in the folds of wide sleeves, up over his head.

"Looks like Ah Fat is taking a nap" said Heath.

Awakened by the sound of nearby voices Ah Fat looked up, bleary eyed and disoriented for a minute.

"It's been a velly long day Mr. Heath" he muttered as he rose from his chair.

"Ah Fat, there's a young man here who could use something to eat to tide him over until breakfast. Could you fix him up?" asked Charles Heath.

"Ah, I tink so", answered Ah Fat, "you likee some blead and cheese? I makee you some tea?"

"That would be wonderful" said Dan as he thanked Charles Heath and the cook. Pointing to the roll of bedding slung over Dan's back Heath commented,

"You have your bedroll with you, I see, so you may stretch out in front of the fire there, if you wish. We'll find something better tomorrow. See you at breakfast." And with that Charles Heath was gone.

Dan thanked Ah Fat for his sandwich and tea, and while he ate, the cook stoked up the fire in the fireplace from a pile of large birch logs stacked close by.

"I velly tired, go to sleep now, see you tomollow" said the Chinese man as he put his hand on the doorknob of his bedroom, just off the kitchen.

Refreshed and rejuvenated from his meal Dan went outside to watch the arrival of the cattle.

Even from where he sat inside the house he had heard them coming for the past half an hour, the low rumble of many hooves on the hard ground, and the whistling and shouting of the cowboys as they herded the cattle along.

It was pitch dark as the great sound reached the ranch, and the open gate leading into the corral. At this same time two or three men carrying lariat ropes came out of a small log cabin behind the main house, to assist in herding the cattle into the corral. Such loud whooping and whistling of the cowboys, mingled with the lowing of many cattle, Dan had never heard before.

He noticed that the animals were all wet, and realized they must have swum the nearby river. Just as they were about to close the gate, Jerome Harper arrived, driving a large white cow with long horns.

"She had wandered into the pasture for a feed" he shouted.

Most herds of cattle had a white cow to lead them on a long drive. Distinguished from the brown, red, and black cattle, the white cow was used over and over, to guide the herds across a river, or over rough ground. Usually the white cow would find her way back home after the drive was over, but in this instance, where the herd had come from hundreds of miles away, it would be kept for a return drive.

Dan slept soundly before the fireplace that night, and woke up hearing many voices all about him. It was Mrs. Boyd and her family of several children, who were eating breakfast in the kitchen.

"Hello there young man" it's time to get up. I trust you slept well." she said as she saw Dan stir from his blankets.

As he arose and looked around the room he met the gaze of Willie, a boy about the same age as himself.

47

Then there was Henry, possibly about fourteen, Mary Anne, a lot older, Alice, a girl in her early teens, Agnes, a pretty girl of about sixteen, and little Ida, about eight.

It would appear that neither Mr. Boyd nor his partner Charles Heath would tolerate any children at the table in the dining room, so they always ate in the kitchen with their mother.

"You can wash in the basin out in the lobby, Dan, and then come back here and have some porridge." said Mrs. Boyd.

CHAPTER 4

A Winter of Experiences

To reach the lobby of the roadhouse, Dan had to go through the dining room. There he came across a dozen men, mostly hired laborers, cowboys, and one or two freighters, who sat eating breakfast at a long table down the center of the room. Serving the food was Ah Fat, assisted by a younger Chinese man named Foo.

Seated at the head of the table was Charles Heath, and to his left, a middle aged man with dark hair and a beard.

"Ah, here is our young man from Newfoundland," announced Charles Heath, "This is Daniel McDermott. Dan, I would like you to meet my partner John Boyd,

"How do you do, Sir," said Dan, shaking Boyd's hand.

"Charles has been telling me about you, Dan. You have done well to have come so far from your home without any serious mishaps, especially your trip on a barge down the Fraser River."

"Yes, there were some very scary moments." replied Dan who was not recalling the terrifying moments in the rapids and canyons of the river, but of the homosexual man Owen, who had assaulted him.

"We could use a stable hand out at the barn, if that would suit you." offered Boyd.

"That would be fine", replied Dan, "anything at all, just to keep warm and to pay for my keep until spring, Sir."

"You can move your things into the room where the cowboys sleep, in the 2nd barn," mentioned Mr. Heath, "there should be an empty bunk there."

"Thank you Sir." replied Dan.

On inspection Dan found the stables in dire need of cleaning, and set to work with a manure fork and wheelbarrow. Housed in the barn were two riding horses; one was a fat old mare that nipped Dan as he worked around her stall.

"Now now old girl, no need to be aggressive with me, I'll do you no harm". The other, a sleek young gelding of Arabian descent was quite friendly, and whinnied when Dan gave him some oats.

'They probably use this one for emergencies, when they need to get somewhere in a hurry' thought Dan.

After working outside for nearly two hours Dan put the tools away and went into the house for a drink of water. In the kitchen he found the family gone, but Ah Fat and Foo were there, preparing lunch. On being introduced to Ah Foo Dan. noticed that compared to Ah Fat, he was tall and very slim.

"I come from northern China, Mongolia", he explained, "Ah Fat come from Canton, in the south."

"How long have you been in Canada, Ah Fat?" asked Dan. "Tree year", replied the affable Chinese, "come to find gold, work all summer, long winter no mine, make money cook for Mr. Heath".

That night Dan came to realize that there were many more Chinese in the area besides Ah Fat and Ah Foo.

Walking into the kitchen for an evening snack, he found Ah Fat entertaining five others of his countrymen, all seated around the kitchen table playing Fan tan, a Chinese gambling game. They were all drinking whiskey and rum, taken, presumably, from the roadhouse supply. Suddenly, just as Dan was enjoying watching the Chinese at their games, the kitchen door opened, and in strode John Boyd.

Looking around at what was going on, his facial expression displayed his disapproval. Ah Fat's friends got the message very quickly, and made a quick exit.

"The cost of the liquor you and your friends have consumed here tonight will be taken out of your wages, Ah Fat. I do not object to you having your friends here to visit, but no more than three at one time please, and make sure you buy your own liquor."

Ah Fat's friends lived in a Chinese community of miners on the Swift River, a tributary of the Cottonwood River, not far from the Cottonwood ranch.

"You likee meet my flends?" Ah Fat asked Dan.

"Yes, I would like to meet your friends, we could go some afternoon when we're not at work." suggested Dan. Ah Foo looked with disapproval at this suggestion. When the two Chinese men were alone Ah Foo remarked to Ah Fat,

"Do you think that is such a good idea, to take young Dan down to the village?"

51

"What harm can it do? he seems a very likeable young man." replied Ah Fat.

"It might shock him to see how some of our countrymen live."

"I don't think you can shock that young fellow, he's come all this way from his home on the other side of Canada; he must be hardened by now." assured Ah Fat.

"If you say so" said Ah Foo.

It was a week later when after having received permission to take the afternoon off, that Dan and the two Chinese men left Cottonwood ranch and walked along a trail leading southeast towards the Swift River. Dan carried his rifle under his arm, incase they came across some game. As they walked through the woods beside the river, a cold wind rustled the leaves of the birch and Cottonwood trees, now almost bare of their golden splendor.

"Pretty soon snow come", remarked Ah Fat, fastening the 'frogs' on his jacket.

Here and there were small meadows where a harvest of grass had been cut that summer, gathered in piles and stacked, each one surrounded by a log enclosure.

"This all belong to John Boyd" explained Ah Fat, "moose and deer try to get in to the stacks in the winter, if they can." he explained further.

About two miles further on they entered a narrow valley through which the river ran and where a number of little log cabins dotted the hillsides.

Closest to the river was a larger log building, and as they came up to it Dan could see red and gold placards with Chinese characters, on both sides of the doorway.

"This our Tong house, we all meet here", explained Ah Fat. As they hesitated outside the building several other Chinese men emerged from the nearby cabins to join them.

Ah Fat, who was obviously very familiar with the men, introduced Dan, and explained that he had come to visit the village. Ah Fat also introduced Dan to Ah Ching, the head man, who spoke very good English. After bowing, Ah Ching said to Dan.

"Please enter our Tong house," and to another Chinese man he mentioned,

"We will serve tea to our visitor."

Inside the Tong house Dan immediately detected the unfamiliar but not unpleasant scent of incense, burning from sticks placed in an urn before a large platform, on the far end of the room. Sitting on a bench with Ah Fat and Ah Foo, Dan observed several others who also sat on a rug. He inquired of Ah Ching,

"What is a tong?"

It is a society of Chinese men." Ching replied.

"This tong was formed to help the Chinese living here in the Cariboo, to help them find work and be able to live decently in this foreign country. We are affiliated with a larger society in China."

Just then two young Chinese boys arrived carrying trays of porcelain cups, a large teapot, and a plate of Chinese cakes. The cups were round, without handles, and decorated in a blue and yellow pattern. Ching poured the tea, which was green, and had a delicate aroma and flavour of jasmine..

On sampling one of the several delicious looking little cakes, Dan decided they were made of a dough-like pastry with an almond flavoured filling.

Ching explained to Dan that there were as many as thirty Chinese men living and working in the neighborhood, and that they had come from China to find gold in 1859.

"Have you found lots of gold?" asked Dan.

The men looked at each other at this question, not knowing how to respond.

"We have experienced much prejudice and jealousy from the Europeans, so we cannot answer your question, as it might hurt our cause; I hope you will understand." said Ching.

While Dan thought about the response, he said to himself

'They wouldn't be here if they were NOT finding gold'

After some time spent drinking tea, eating cakes and enjoying some pleasant conversation, Ah Fat signaled to Dan and Ah Foo that it was time for them to leave.

"Foo and I must get back in time to cook dinner at the roadhouse, and Dan must get back to feed the horses." he explained to Ah Ching.

"Come again, now that you know the way", said Ah Ching to Dan.

Ah Fat's prediction of snow was correct, for only a week later a blanket of several inches of dry powdery snow fell, making everything look clean and bright.

It was late one evening just as John Boyd was about to lock up and go to bed, when a freight wagon arrived in the barnyard at the Cottonwood farm.

A freezing rain was coming down hard, driven by a strong wind that had swept up the valley from the west.

As John stood waiting for the freighter to arrive at the door of the house, a thick mist rising from the ground created a dense fog over everything, and hid the presence of the figure on the doorstep.

"Good evening John" said the man as Boyd let him in. It was Harry Morfittt, on his way from Alexandria, to sell his produce at Williams Creek

"Come in and shut the door; you're soaking wet." said John in an impatient tone of voice.

"Yes, yes" replied Harry, removing his coat, and giving it a good shake.

"I suppose you have a full load of goods, as usual."

Yes, and I know it's late, but I would like to stay the night and then go on early in the morning."

"We have a full house tonight, Harry. Your usual room is taken."

"That's alright, I'll sleep in the barn." replied Harry.

"Come then" said Boyd, "take off your wet things, and I'll make you a cup of hot tea."

Leading the way to the kitchen John noticed that the cook had gone to bed, but that the fire was still burning in the grate. Removing a stove lid, he placed the kettle over the hot coals, and waited for it to boil.

How was your hay crop this year, John?" inquired the freighter.

"Good, the main fields are all cut and stacked" replied John, "only the swamp meadows, such as Foster Flats, have been too wet to cut. We may have to cut those on the ice."

"Have you heard any more about the building of the road? I hear that the Royal Engineers are going to change the survey again." mentioned Harry, taking out his cigarette rollings.

"Oh no," replied John, "not again!"

"Yes, apparently they are going to cross the Cottonwood River on part of Smith's ranch."

"Ho ho" exclaimed John Boyd, "but wouldn't that would be a conflict of interest?"

"Yes, I agree" replied Harry "but what can you do."

"If the road is built by that route, we will have to move the location of this roadhouse. It will mean an enormous expense to my partner Charles Heath and myself." replied John, remorsefully.

As John poured the tea and Harry sat warming himself beside the oven door, neither of them heard young Dan enter the house by way of the cook's entrance. He had been in bed when he remembered his sweater that he had left on the railing of the main staircase.

As he passed through the dining room he could hear John Boyd talking to someone in the kitchen. He could also hear another sound, of someone coming down the back stairs at the far end of the dining room. Realizing that he should not have been lurking around at such a late hour, Dan darted behind the broad leaves of the tall aspidistra plant standing in a corner, and out of curiosity, looked to see who it was on the stairs.

It was Agnes, the pretty sixteen year old.

The several daughters of John and Janet Boyd, Mary Anne, Agnes, Lily, and little Ida occupied two of the four upstairs bedrooms. While most were asleep at this time, Agnes lay, still fully clothed, on her single cot. On hearing Harry Morfitt's voice downstairs, she quietly and stealthily arose and made her way out onto the landing, and started down the back stairs. From experience she knew every stair, and just where to tread to avoid the squeaks. As she reached the bottom step, she paused to listen.

'Ah ha' said Dan to himself, 'she is hiding her presence.' He waited to see what would happen next.

"How are things at home, Harry?" asked John as he poured him another cup of tea.

"Just as much of a turmoil as ever." Harry replied. "My wife refuses to live with me, so I am having a house built in Quesnelle, where she can live, and look after the children while they go to school. Only young Henry and Roddie are on the farm with me now."

By this time John and Harry had left the kitchen, John heading for the bedroom he shared with his wife at the far end of the house, while Harry took up his coat and left for the barn, by way of the kitchen door.

Agnes had obviously heard Harry leave the house, for then Dan saw her dart across the kitchen to the door, following after him.

'Ah ha' said Dan to himself, 'something fishy going on here!' Gathering up his sweater from the newel post on the main staircase, he returned to his bed in the second barn. He knew he had witnessed something clandestine, but it was something he would keep to himself.

As Agnes reached the barn door she could hear Harry climbing up the ladder to the loft. Following behind him, Harry could hear her approaching.

"You are a brave one to risk coming up here. If your father finds out, we will both be crucified. You can't stay here with me, we will be found out." he chided.

"Oh Harry" Agnes crooned, "I know you want me, just as I want you. I have known it ever since you took my hand at Mary Anne's engagement party.

"Yes, I know, but it is still not right; I am a married man."

"But your wife is a shrew, and will not have you." said Agnes as she settled into Harry's arms in the hay.

"You are so mature, Harry, so sophisticated, not at all like the other young men who come by." whispered Agnes as she held Harry close, and stroked his dark, curly hair. Harry's resistance broke down at this point.

"Yes, it is true, I have wanted you" he panted, as he thrust his face down onto her ample breasts. As they held each other close Agnes tore open the buttons on Harry's shirt, while he began to undress her. Soon they were both naked, fondling and kissing ardently. When Harry entered her, Agnes felt a sharp pain, but the accompanying ecstasy was so all encompassing it was soon forgotten.

It was very early in the morning when Agnes awoke, dressed herself and stole back to the house. As she entered the kitchen door she was greeted by a blast of warm air, and found the cook preparing breakfast.

Ah Fat gave Agnes a very quizzical look, for it was not usual to see Miss Agnes up so early.

At breakfast one morning John Boyd asked Dan if he would accompany him to feed the cattle.

"Cattle are not like horses", he explained, "they do not dig through the snow for the grass, so they have to be fed."

As Dan walked toward the barn he encountered the cattle that had gathered behind the fence, close to the barn. The herd of about fifty steers and heifers of mixed breed were all bawling to be fed.

Together Dan and John Boyd hitched a team of big work horses to a 'slip', a large flat wooden board, mounted on sleigh runners, and went out over the snow into the field, to the nearest hay stack. The cattle followed close behind, bawling, and as they approached the stack Dan had to fight his way through them to reach the fence surrounding the haystack.

While Dan let the rails down, John Boyd moved the team in beside the stack.

"Put the rails back up" Boyd hollered to Dan as the cattle began to move in. While the cattle waited impatiently, Dan and John Boyd used pitchforks to send the hay down on to the slip.

Once the hay was fed out in little piles over the meadow, the cattle went to feeding, and all was quiet, save the steady sound of rustling hay, and the munching of many cattle.

As Dan grew more familiar with the operations of the ranch and roadhouse, he became aware of the competition between Boyd and Heath of the Cottonwood farm, and the several other roadhouses situated between Quesnellemouth and Barkerville.

One in particular, Pine Grove or Edward's House, as it was also known, a few miles east of Cottonwood, was a real threat to Boyd's business.

Mrs. Edwards and her married daughter Elsie were known to be excellent cooks, serving almost gourmet meals, compared to the plain fare served by the Chinese cook at Cottonwood.House.

Much to the annoyance of John Boyd, he realized this was taking business away from him.

On more than one occasion Dan had heard John Boyd grumble about the excellence of the Edwards' table, and how their dining room was full at every meal.

"I have just heard that the Edwards' recently catered to a party of businessmen from Victoria" he announced to his wife.

"Perhaps I should take charge of the cooking" Janet Boyd suggested to her husband.

Nonsense, my dear, that won't be necessary." her husband replied.

Janet Boyd had come from a good family on the San Juan Islands, and was an accomplished cook and housekeeper, but unless the Chinese cook took sick, her husband would not expect her to take charge of the kitchen.

It was obvious to Dan that John Boyd knew that Edwards was carrying a mortgage, and was just waiting for him to default on the payment. Then he could buy the property, and eliminate the competition.

That winter, while delivering some hay to Edward's ranch Dan overheard a conversation between Harry Hamilton, Elsie's husband, and Ned Edwards, Elsie's father.

"Are you going to be able to pay the mortgage this month?" Harry asked Ned.

"I don't know" replied Ned "business has been so slow lately, I may have to ask for an extension this month, I do hope Mr. Hoffmier will be reasonable." added Ned.

It was true, thought Dan to himself, there hadn't been many travelers for some time, and with the Cariboo wagon road unfinished, and blocked, sometimes for days after a heavy snowfall, it was no wonder.

"Well I wish you luck" said Harry to his father-in-law "That old skinflint is never reasonable."

Dan had heard that Mr. Hoffmeir was the money lender at Quesnellemouth, and also that his reputation of foreclosing on his client's mortgages was well

61

known.

As Dan went into Edwards' House to deliver the bill for the hay, he was amazed to see such a luxurious interior; the expensive furniture and fittings, so different from Boyd's rough and ready house. The carpets in the lobby were Persian, and of the finest quality and design; there were also crystal chandeliers hanging from the ceiling, and silver candlestick holders mounted on the walls.

'Of course' mused Dan to himself, 'Cottonwood is a ranch, with a roadhouse, while Edwards is only a roadside inn and restaurant, entirely dependant on the public; why, they don't put up enough hay to feed a few head of horses, let alone a herd of cattle.

It was late in February that year, and snow had fallen to a depth of several feet. On the trails only the constant use of sleighs had kept them open.

After a heavy fall, it was sometimes necessary to help the horses to get through the heavy drifts by shoveling the snow off the trail

Towards dusk, Dan had been out at the barn, putting some more hay into the stalls, when he heard the sound of harness jingling close by.

'Someone is arriving' he thought.

Just as he was about to look around the corner of the barn, he practically ran into a large white and tan workhorse, its harness broken, and the single trees dragging on the ground.

"Hello there, big fella, where did you come from?" said Dan. The horse snorted and looked up, smelling the fresh hay in the barn.

"I guess you're hungry aren't you? well come on in." said Dan as he opened the barn door and allowed the horse to enter.

Walking over to the house, Dan found Mr. Heath, and told him about the horse. As they walked back to the barn, a second horse, similar to the first, appeared.

"There has been an accident somewhere, and these horses have managed to get loose from their rigging" declared Mr. Heath. "we must go up, or down the trail, to investigate."

On leading the second horse into the barn, Dan and Mr. Heath lost no time in harnessing up a riding horse to a small sled, and moved out onto the trail.

From the tracks left by the large horses in the deep snow, it left no doubt that they had come down the steep hill a mile or two east of the ranch.

"Keep watch for more pieces of the harness, Dan," shouted Heath, as they followed the tracks.

More than a mile further on, about half way up the steep hill, they came upon a terrible sight.

Two large work horses from the original four, still in harness, lay resting in the snow, the warm air from their nostrils forming a white fog as it hit the cold, winter air. Close by, a large freight sleigh, it's runners sticking straight up in the air, lay upside down in the deep snow.

"I wonder where the driver is?" Dan called to Mr. Heath.

"I hate to suggest", he answered, "but I think he is

probably under the sleigh"

"We'll have to get these two horses up, and encourage them to pull the sleigh over to the bank. Perhaps then we can look underneath for the driver." suggested Mr. Heath.

Untying the straps holding the two big horses from the harness, Mr. Heath and Dan persuaded the two animals to rise up out of their beds in the snow

"I wonder how long they have been here", said Dan.

"Probably most of the day, as it would be some time before the other two horses could get down the hill to our barn."

It took a lot of encouragement to get the horses up, but finally, when Dan tempted them with some hay from a bag on the sleigh, they got up.

"Now," said Heath, if we can get enough leather together, we could fasten it to the double trees there, and start moving the sleigh."

It took a while, but finally they were able to move the sleigh over to the edge of the trail.

"The driver must have lost control on the steep hill, and jumped off on the wrong side" concluded Mr. Heath. Just as Dan was about to climb down to take a look under the sleigh, they heard a series of thumps, as several heavy barrels fell out and rolled off down the bank into the snow. Then something heavier fell out, and landed in the deep snow. Mr. Heath climbed down the bank to take a look.

More than a mile further on, about half way up the steep hill, they came across a terrible sight.

"It's Antoine Parody, the freighter" he called. "He's been crushed to death. I remember now, he was due to deliver some barrels of beer today."

"Let's try to get his body up out of the snow, and onto the sleigh", suggested Mr. Heath.

The snow where the body lay was at least three feet deep, and in order to carry it out to the trail, the two men had first to shovel a path.

An hour later, and as darkness fell, they carried the body over to the sleigh, and heaved it up on to the deck.

After resting for a few minutes Mr. Heath, who was still out of breath, suggested,

"Dan, you take the horses down to the barn, while I drive the sleigh back "

"Yes sir" said Dan, as he gathered up the horse's harness, and drove the large animals through the snow to the trail, and down the steep hill to the barn at Cottonwood Ranch.

Antoine Parody, the freighter, was a Mexican, who, at one time had worked for the Hudson's Bay Co. before the gold rush. For a number of years now, he had been in the employ of Abraham Barlow, a Quesnelle merchant, delivering everything from hay, feed, and roadhouse supplies between Quesnelle and Williams Creek.

On notifying Mr. Barlow of the accident, Mr. Heath and John Boyd received a visit from him, when he arrived to view the body, and to reimburse them for having rescued the dead man, the horses, and the equipment.

With below zero temperatures that winter, the body had frozen stiff, and as the ground was also frozen, the corpse was kept at the Cottonwood Ranch, in a box, in the blacksmith shop.

When the ground thawed that next spring, Antoine Parody was buried in the little graveyard at the foot of the long hill, which afterwards was named Mexican Hill.

It was just after breakfast one early spring morning when a black man rode in to the ranch.

"Good morning Sir" he called out to Mr Heath, who met him by the barn.

"I am looking for a friend of mine, a Canadian named Morgan Blessing. He was to have reached Barkerville a week ago, but has not been seen by anyone I have spoken with. I wondered if he might have stopped here. I have mentioned the disappearance to the police in Barkerville, but they are so short handed, that it would be a while before they would have time to investigate."

"Can you describe him" replied Mr. Heath, "we get a lot of men stopping here for a meal, or to stay overnight, but if you could tell me what he looks like, I might remember."

"Actually, he was traveling with another man, a neer do well, well, lets put it this way, one with a questionable reputation. I never should have let my friend travel with the man. Morgan is fairly tall, well built, with fair hair. He is about fifty years of age."

"This traveling companion of Morgan Blessing, did he get to Barkerville"? asked Mr. Heath.

"Yes, his name is James Barry, and when I asked him about Morgan, he claimed that he had stopped overnight somewhere, because his feet were sore. There is only Beaver Pass House, and the hotel at Van Winkle, where he could have stayed over, but no one there has seen him." mentioned Mr. Moses

Dan, who had been cleaning out one of the stalls in the barn, overheard the conversation. 'I don't remember ever seeing such a man' Dan said to himself. 'A neer do well, eh? It doesn't sound too good.

Wandering out of the barn with a manure fork in his hand, Dan stood near Mr. Moses' horse, so that he could join in the conversation,

"If I may be so bold as to make a suggestion, Sir, "said Dan, "if I were you, I would go back along the trail to where he, that is your friend Mr. Blessing, was last seen, and make a thorough search around there."

"Are you suggesting that Blessing has been murdered?" asked Mr. Moses.

"Well, he doesn't seem to be anywhere," remarked Mr. Heath, "so that is the next possibility."

"I do intend to look along the trail" replied Mr.Moses. "I don't suppose you could spare this young man to help me search for a few hours, could you? I would be willing to pay you." suggested Mr. Moses

"If he finishes cleaning out the barn he could go

for a few hours; do you want to help, Dan?" Mr. Heath asked.

Dan thought this would be an exciting thing to do, something quite apart from his rather monotonous routine at the roadhouse.

"I'll just be a few minutes, Sir" said Dan to Mr. Moses, then turning to Charles Heath he asked "which horse shall I take, Sir?"

"Blackie, the young gelding" replied Heath. Collecting up the remainder of the dung and soiled hay from the barn, Dan deposited it in a manure pile out in the barnyard, and then saddled up the horse.

Before leaving with Mr. Moses, Dan stopped in at the kitchen of the roadhouse, where Ah Fat the cook gathered up a lunch for him of several pieces of buttered bread and a hunk of cooked meat, and wrapped them up in a flour sack.

"Take a coat with you Dan, it looks like rain." advised the cook.

It was a good twelve miles east from Cottonwood to Edward's House, where Mr. Moses had last seen Morgan Blessing, and during their ride Moses gave Dan a lot of additional information.

"I got to know Morgan Blessing when I lived in Victoria, infact it was Morgan who persuaded me to set up a business in Barkerville. I have a barber shop there." At this point there was a pause of several minutes as Moses got out a hankerchief, dabbed his eyes, and coughed.

"You see, I was an escaped slave from the Caribbean, and Morgan was a part of the underground railway, as it was called, that helped slaves to escape. Morgan was financially able to assist in the movement having done very well in the California gold rush. What makes me really suspicious of James Barry, the gambler, is that Morgan had a beautiful gold nugget pin, that he wore in his cravat. A few days ago, one of the Hurdy Gurdy girls came into my shop in Barkerville, and showed me that exact same pin. She said that James Barry had given it to her. Morgan would never have given that pin away, it was quite precious to him." Once again Moses had to use his hankerchief.

A little over an hour later they were talking to Mr. Edwards, owner of Pine Grove House.

"Yes," he said when Moses approached him, "I bloody well remember you that day, Mr Moses, and your two companions also."

"After leaving your restaurant I left Blessing and James Barry, while I hurried on to Barkerville. Blessing has not been seen since, so we are looking for him." explained Moses.

"Oh bloody hell" said Edwards, "are you sure he didn't stop off somewhere?"

"I have checked every possible place, but no one has seen him."

"That sounds bloody well suspicious." put in Edwards, "have you checked along the trail past here?"

"We are going to do that now." Moses told Mr. Edwards.

"I would come and bloody well help you look"

70

added Mr. Edwards, "but I have to look after some guests here."

"That's alright," replied Moses, "I have young Dan with me, from Cottonwood House, to help, but first I had to check with you."

"Would you bloody well care to stop for a drink before you start your search?" asked Edwards.

While Mr. Moses sat in the saloon at Pine Grove House, Dan sat on the fence outside, and ate his lunch. He thought about the probability that Blessing had been murdered. Actually, there was every reason for the gambler to commit murder.

Morgan Blessing probably had a fat wallet, and there was that gold nugget pin he wore. But what would the murderer have used for a weapon? A revolver? No, that would make a loud noise that might be heard. A blow to the head with a heavy object such as a rock? quite possibly. Or perhaps the murderer had a knife, or a dagger. That type of person would probably carry a knife.

If James Barry killed Morgan Blessing, what would he have used to bury the body? Would he have had a shovel? No, he was a gambler, not a miner. Ahh, but Mr. Blessing could have had a shovel in his pack, as he was a miner. Having killed Blessing, Barry would have been in a hurry to get away from the site, so the grave was probably very shallow, and easily detected.'

Just then Moses came out of the house, and climbed on to his horse. As they started back along the trail to make a close examination, Moses directed Dan to take the lower side, while he looked on the upper.

About a mile from Edward's House, the trail passed through a dense, forested area, where the sun seldom shone, and here Dan got off the horse and tied it, while he walked slowly along, examining the underbrush. Just then Mr. Moses arrived, and dismounted.

"I could not see you, so I thought I had better come and look with you." he said.

Suddenly Dan detected an area of disturbance where he stood in the brush, where someone had recently made a fire, and cleared a small space of dead branches.

"Come and look over here, Mr. Moses" Dan called. Together they poked around through the dense underbrush, when suddenly Dan saw it, a grave size pile of recently disturbed dirt, covered over with dead branches.

"This looks a lot like a grave, Sir," said Dan, pointing it out to Moses.

"What shall we use to dig?" asked Moses.

Dan was wondering the same thing, when suddenly nearby, he spied a wooden handle, sticking up through the dirt. Stepping over to it, he pulled up a short handled miner's prospecting shovel.

"The murderer left the shovel," said Dan as he began to dig. Moses had removed the pile of dead branches, and while waiting for Dan, had taken out his hankerchief again.

Digging down about two feet through the soft dirt, Dan came across the body, so recently buried that de-

72

composition had not begun.

Moses identified it as that of Morgan Blessing, and Dan shoveled some dirt and rocks over the body again, for fear of wolves or coyotes devouring it.

As each of them started back home, Dan to the west, and Mr. Moses to the east, Mr. Moses thanked Dan for his help,

"Come to town when you need a haircut, Dan, and I will accommodate you."

Back in Barkerville, Mr. Moses reported finding the body of Morgan Blessing to the police, and insisted that they find James Barry immediately, and arrest him.

As it happened, the Overland Telegraph Co. had installed a line to Williams Creek that year, and the police were able to send word of the wanted man to various stations in the south.

James Barry was arrested just as he was boarding a sternwheel ship at Yale, and was brought back to Richfield to stand trial.

Two months later both Moses and Daniel McDermott were served with writs of subpoena, to appear as witnesses at the fall assizes.

CHAPTER 5

Road to the Goldfields

With spring in the air, and the presence of several Swallows building nests out at the barn, Dan began to feel that he should be moving on. He was anxious to get to the gold fields to try his hand at mining. On a bright and sunny morning Dan decided this was the day he would leave Cottonwood.

'How would he get there?' he wondered. Williams Creek was a good thirty-five miles away, to the east, and he did not relish walking all that distance. When Dan first arrived at Cottonwood, Mr. Boyd had noticed his worn out shoes, and gave him a pair of work boots to wear.

'I'm not going to wear these out if I can help it,' he said to himself.

Recalling that there had been one or two freighters at the breakfast table that morning, Dan made his way to the barn, where he knew they would be getting their wagons and horses ready for the road. Among several others Dan recognized Harry Morfitt.

"Could I catch a ride with you to Williams Creek, Sir," Dan asked, as he tied a bag of oats on to Harry's wagon.

"Why yes, I would be glad to have your company. It's a long, lonely trip with out someone to talk to. You can be my swamper."

"What is a swamper?" asked Dan.

"A swamper looks after the horses, feeds and waters them, and generally chore around with anything that needs attention," said Harry.

"Just up my alley," said Dan. "I will begin by telling you that your horses are anxious to get moving."

"How do you know that?" asked Harry.

"When they start prancing up and down in their harness, it is a sign of restlessness."

"Well, I will have to be more observant from now on." mused Harry who had been working with horses for most of his life.

Harry Morfitt was a very young man when he first arrived in the Cariboo from his home in Pembroke, Ontario. Before long he had taken up three hundred and twenty acres of land in the Alexandria area, thirty miles south of Quesnellemouth.

There he had built a house, and married Winnie Moddie, a sixteen year old girl from Scotland.

Over the following fifteen years nine children were born, five boys, and four girls.

As the family increased, religious differences began to tear the marriage apart, Winnie was a devout Catholic, and Harry, a member of the Presbyterian church.

When they were first married a pact was made between them, that when the children came the girls would be brought up as Catholics, and the boys would follow their father, as Presbyterians.

This arrangement was broken on more than one occasion when Harry, who made most of his living transporting grain and produce to the gold fields, arrived home unexpectedly to find a Catholic priest baptizing his sons.

Winnie resented the fact that Harry was away from the ranch for long periods of time, and that she had to plant the garden, and supervise hired help to work in the fields.

Harry insisted that he could not trust anyone else to conduct his business. He was acutely reminded of what had happened a few years earlier to his neighbours, the owners of the Australian ranch

It was at the close of their first year of operation, and after clearing a field, and breaking their backs, they produced an acre of potatoes and turnips.

To market their produce they made a deal with a passing freighter to take it toWilliams Creek, where he would sell it, and pay them on his return trip.

The freighter took the vegetables, but did not return with the money. Apparently he had sold their produce, and then left the country by an alternate route. At that time it meant a long trip to report such dishonest dealings, and consequently Andrew Olson and his partners almost starved. that winter

When Dan went to say goodbye to the Boyd family he was actually sorry to be leaving, but he was also excited about what the future held for him.

Over the winter he had learned that while John

Boyd was strict in his demands, he was also a very generous man, even with the children of the family, and believed that if anyone worked for him, even Mrs. Boyd, that they should be paid. As an accountant by profession, John Boyd kept a very close eye on his financial dealings.

Every evening after supper he would be at his desk in the lobby of the roadhouse, entering the day's trans-actions in to a ledger.

The day before he left Dan spoke to Boyd, informed him of his departure, and requested him to write a short reference for him.

"It will help a lot when I go looking for a job." he said

"Why certainly, Dan," said John, we have found you to be a hard and honest worker."

"Thank you Sir." replied Dan

As Dan climbed up on to Harry Morfitt's wagon that morning, Charles Heath and the cook Ah Fat came down to the barn to see him off.

"I am sure you will come to see us when you can, and remember, if you ever need our help, let us know." said Heath.

Ah Fat had a package for him, tied up in a flour sack;

"Here Dan, some lunch" he said, as he passed the parcel up to Dan, "to keep your stomach quiet."

"I shall really miss your cooking, Ah Fat." Dan said, as he gave the teary eyed Oriental a hug.

As Harry and Dan journeyed along the trail towards

the gold fields, the wagon got stuck several times in deep mud holes. When this happened they had to get down off the wagon, and while Dan pushed with all his might, Harry took the reins out in front of the wagon, and encouraged the team to pull hard.

In one such hole, where they were stuck for several hours, they had to unload most of the freight by the side of the trail, so that the team could pull the wagon out.

Every few miles they came across parties of men mining on the creeks, and at one they noticed particularly, where the miners had dammed up Lightning Creek to take out the gold lying on the bottom.

Perched on the hillsides and protected by forests of Pine and Spruce, the miners had pitched their tents, while others had built log cabins.

Ever since leaving Cottonwood the trail had led up hill, and off in the distance they could see high mountains.

"It is up in the mountains where the big gold nuggets are found." Harry mentioned to Dan.

"Don't they find nuggets in the creeks?" asked Dan.

"Only small nuggets, but probably great quantities of them. It has to do with the glaciers that came through here many eons ago." explained Harry.

It was getting late in the evening when they reached the wide valley of Beaver Pass. They had covered eighteen miles of rough trail from Cottonwood, and the horses were getting tired.

On reaching Beaver Pass House, the freighter

stopped and sold some oats and wheat to "Scotty" Georgeson, the owner of the roadhouse.

"Have ye any carrots or Neeps to sell me Harry?" asked the Scot. "I've no had the chance to get to Richfield for a time."

"Yes, will you take fifty pounds of each?" asked Harry.

"What are Neeps?" asked Dan.

It's a Scotch word for turnips" replied Harry.

The altitude and the frequent frosts during the summer in that region, prevented the growing of a garden, so all vegetables had to be imported.

"Are ye a mind to stay the night?" asked Scotty, "I've got a good Caribou stew on, and if I add some veggies to it, it will be even better."

The roadhouse, a large, single story log cabin built close to Lightning Creek, had been constructed only two years before, and was not yet completed.

At one end of the structure was a large open faced fireplace, where logs as large as one foot in diameter, and four feet in length, were burned.

Hanging over the fire were iron rods, where food such as oatmeal porridge and stew could be cooked in iron pots

"Did you shoot the Caribou yourself?" asked Dan as he arranged his blankets out in front of the fireplace.

"Actually it was my partner George who shot it up near Van Winkle; when it paused at the creek to take a drink. A large brute it was, with antlers, well, as you can see up there" he said pointing proudly to the trophy.

Dan had noticed the broad, multi pronged antlers displayed on the wall across from the fireplace.

Up early the next morning, the sun was peeping out from behind grey clouds as they left the roadhouse and headed east for another ten miles to Van Winkle, a small mining community on Lightning Creek.

Here they stopped at the back door of the store, and while Harry spoke with Mr. McCaffrey, the owner of the hotel, post office, and store, Dan took the horses down to the creek for a drink. As he stood waiting for the animals to satisfy their thirst, he looked around him.

The settlement of Van Winkle, containing about a dozen log buildings, had been built in a narrow valley at the confluence of Van Winkle and Lightning Creeks.

When the first miners came over the hills from Antler Creek in 1861 they had found very rich deposits of gold at the site, and a settlement began there. Now, several years later, the hillsides were bare, and only a sea of stumps remained of the trees cut down by the miners, to build small log cabins and pit props, for the underground mines nearby.

It seemed a rather gloomy place to Dan.

'The valley is so narrow here' he thought, 'I'll bet the sun seldom shines, except perhaps in the middle of summer.'

Having concluded their business at the store, Dan and Harry went into the restaurant for a meal.

Harry and Dan reach Van Winkle, on Lightning Creek

Waiting on them was a young, blonde, European woman with her little son, about two years old. After a few minutes Mr. McCaffrey himself appeared and sat down at the table with Dan and Harry.

"This is my wife and son," he said in a thick Scottish brogue, referring to the attractive blonde waitress and the little boy. She was an American that McCaffrey had met in California.

"How do you like living up north here, Mr. McCaffrey?" inquired Dan.

"There's lots of money to be made from the miners, and because of the gold rush" he replied "but I am going to give up running the post office."

"Why is that?" asked Harry, as he swallowed the last morsel of his dinner. "Is it too much work?"

"No, not really" said McCaffrey playing with the large nugget ring that he wore on his left hand.

"It's because the government does not pay me. When I first started two years ago I was paid regularly, but I have not had a cheque now for six months."

From Van Winkle Harry Morfitt and Daniel McDermott traveled east again, past a prosperous looking roadhouse at Dunbar Flats, kept by Janet Allen; through the Milk Ranch pass, across Jack of Clubs Creek, and around Groundhog Lake, for another fifteen miles to the community of Richfield, on Williams Creek.

All along the way they came across parties of miners working their claims in the creeks, and on the hillsides

At one camp, a man came running out of a cabin,

82

shouting at the top of his lungs

"Stop, stop, I want to buy some vegetables."

It appeared that he and his comrades were sick, and one man had died of scurvy, a condition resulting from the lack of vegetables in their diet.

On pulling the horses to a halt, Dan got down off the wagon and held the horses, while Harry sold several bags of potatoes, cabbages, and turnips to the crazed men. One man was so anxious, he grabbed a potato and ate it raw in front of them.

As they neared Richfield they could hardly manoeuvre the horses and wagon through the crowds of miners at work with their endless sluices, flumes and ditches. Further down the street they pulled in at the Hudson's Bay Co. trading store.

"This is the end of the road for you, young man" said Harry to Dan, "You're on your own now. I imagine you could find a 'diggins' somewhere if you just ask around. I enjoyed having you along, you are a smart lad."

"Thanks for the ride, Harry" replied Dan, I have learned a lot about the people and places along the way. I'm sure I will see you again, if not here, then at Cottonwood" he said with a decided wink of his eye. Harry looked startled at this parting remark.

CHAPTER 6

A Rough Beginning in the Goldfields

It was mid afternoon as Harry and Dan reached Williams Creek, and Dan was hungry, not having eaten since lunch.

From outside the Hudson's Bay Co. store, he could see a sign advertising Andrew Kelly's Bake Shop and Lunch House. Strolling up the crowded, muddy, rutted street he was jostled by others, and splattered with mud from passing wagons.

Climbing up the steep stairs off the street he found himself at the door of the restaurant.

Inside, the smoke from many cigars almost choked him as he found his way to the counter.

Waiting his turn behind several other men, Dan searched his pockets for some change.

"What can I get you?" asked the young waiter behind the counter.

"Do you have any soup?" asked Dan.

"Yes, beef or vegetable?"

"Vegetable, please, a large bowl, and a bun too."

"That will be a dollar fifty please" said the cashier."

Dan could hardly believe his ears.

"How much did you say?"

"A dollar and fifty cents." he repeated.

84

"In that case I will change my order, and have just the bun, please."

"A plain bun, or a sweet bun?"

"A sweet bun please" said Dan.

"That will be fifty cents, please. Would you like a cup of coffee too, that would be included with the bun" he added.

"Yes please" said Dan, in a daze. His bit of money was not going to go far here he realized.

'I will have to find myself a job as soon as possible.'

Just as Dan turned from the counter with his coffee and bun to find a seat, a tall, middle aged man with crinkly brown hair bumped into him.

He looked like a working man, or perhaps a miner, dressed in a checkered mackinaw coat, and wearing tall rubber boots.

"Hey there young fella, sorry if I spilled your drink. It's very crowded in here. You could sit with me across the way, if you want."

Dan waited for the man to make his purchase, and then followed him through the noisy throng to a table on the far side of the room. As Bob sat down, he introduced Dan to the man sitting beside him.

"This is Andrew Kelly, the proprietor of this restaurant," he said to Dan, "and my name is Bob Chase. Who might you be?"

"Daniel McDermott from Newfoundland, Sir, I have just arrived on Williams Creek and I hope to try my hand at mining."

"Very ambitious, I must say," said Andrew Kelly.

"Bob Chase here has been working a claim this summer; perhaps he could give you a few pointers."

"Thank you sir, I would appreciate that."

"Would you would like to come out with me to where I am digging a shaft. I can't pay you, but you could share my vitals and help with the work." offered Bob.

"Where are you mining?" asked Dan.

"My claim is on Jack of Clubs Creek, not many miles from here."

"Oh yes, I know now, we passed it on our way here from Cottonwood." Dan was silent for a moment, thinking over the offer.

'I really have nothing to lose' he said to himself, and if this Bob is willing to teach me something, and feed me, I should try it for a spell.'

"When are you leaving town?" asked Dan.

Right away, if you are ready." replied Bob.

"I'm with you then." said Dan.

Bidding Andrew Kelly farewell, Dan followed Bob out of the restaurant, and walked with him down the crowded, muddy road to Mundorf's stables.

"I am having one of my horses shod." said Bob. "You wait here with the wagon and team, while I pick up a parcel. I won't be long." he said as he turned on his heel and disappeared down the street.

As Dan walked into the dimly lit stables, he found the farrier Joseph Mundorf by following the sound of hammering as he pounded the nails into the shoe of a large work horse. A second horse was tethered close by.

"Are these Bob Chase's horses ?" Dan asked

"Yes, they are, and I am nearly finished." he said

While he waited Dan looked up and down the road to see if he could spot Bob returning. There was still no sign of him, but the sound of cowboys herding a dozen cattle along the street, and dogs barking, was coming closer. As they passed by, Dan ducked into the safety of the stables.

"Where are they taking those cattle?" he asked, Mr. Mundorf.

"Over to Ben Von Volkenburgh's holding pens on Bald Mountain. That's where they fatten them up. He also has a butcher shop at the far end of town." replied Mundorf.

Just then Bob Chase turned up carrying a large parcel under his arm. On paying the farrier, Bob called out

"Help me harness the horses, Dan, and we'll get out of here."

The wagon was a rather dilapidated wooden crate that had obviously seen better times, but it followed along behind the team, supposedly still in one piece.

In the back of the wagon a large load of hay had been dumped on top of other supplies necessary to someone living a fair distance from town.

Dan sat up beside Bob on the wagon, as they traveled south along the main trail for about five miles, past Summit Rock, and to the junction of Jack of Clubs

Creek. Turning north they drove along a narrow, rutted trail for another three miles, when suddenly they broke out of the timber and entered a wide, open valley where a large creek ran, and close to it was a small log cabin, and a barn.

"Did you build the cabin and barn yourself Bob?" asked Dan as the horses struggled through the mud.

"No, they were built earlier, by a miner who sold the claim to me."

"Did he find lots of gold here?" asked Dan.

"He showed me some nice nuggets he said he found here."

"How do you know the nuggets came from here?" questioned Dan.

"Because he said so" said Bob in a tiresome tone. "You ask too many questions."

"I'm sorry, I just wondered why you were not doing as well." replied Dan.

As they drew close to the buildings, a large curly haired dog ran out of the barn, barking and wagging its stump of a tail.

"Here we are" said Bob, petting and greeting the dog as it jumped up on to the wagon. "This is home sweet home, and this is my dog "Curly".

"You can put the team away in the barn, Dan, if you will, and find a fork to put the hay down, while I unload the wagon." called Bob as he climbed down off the wagon.

Half an hour later Dan, Bob and Curly were sitting around the fireplace in the cabin, where Bob had started a fire and heated up a pot of beans

"How are you at cooking, Dan" asked Bob.

"Over the winter I watched a Chinese cook at work in Cottonwood House, so I think I could keep from starving if I had to." replied Dan.

"Can you make biscuits?" Bob asked.

"I have never tried, but I think I could."

"They want such an awful price for anything at the restaurants and stores on Williams Creek." continued Bob

"Yes, as I discovered that today." mentioned Dan.

"I was just shocked. I suppose it is the cost of transporting supplies from the south, and of course, the high demand." added Dan.

"Yes" said Bob, I'm running out of cash, and if I don't soon find some gold on this claim, I am going to have to abandon it. It is costing me too much to stay here." confided Bob.

"Could we have a look at what you are doing, Bob?" asked Dan, who was anxious to see how mining was done.

"It's getting late tonight" said Bob, "but tomorrow morning we will go to work, and I'll show you. Right now we need some more wood to keep the fire going, and some water from the creek, before night falls."

As Bob went out to the woodpile, Dan grabbed the two buckets by the cabin door and made his way down to the creek, about fifty feet away.

The snow here had obviously melted very recently, for the short grass and weeds lay flat on the ground, and the whole surface was covered with mouse trails, where they had traveled under the snow all winter.

The Jack of Clubs was a slow moving creek, about three feet wide, and as Dan stepped out on to some big quartz rocks to fill the buckets, he tasted the water. It was heavily mineralized, clear, and tasted like wine.

Back at the cabin once more Dan settled into his blankets, while Bob and Curly went to bed on the single cot in the corner, and soon all were asleep.

It was broad daylight when Dan awoke to the sound of Bob clanging pots, making porridge and coffee beside the fireplace. In the corner by the door Curly was chewing on a big Caribou bone.

"Are there many Caribou around here?" asked Dan as he got dressed.

"They are getting scarce" said Bob "but there are still some in the tall timber to the south. I shot this one last fall, and it is almost all eaten now."

After breakfast they made a lunch and gathered up two shovels, two picks, a coil of rope, and a long wooden ladder.

Hiking along for about a quarter of a mile, they came to the site of Bob's mining shaft.

"The bedrock on this creek, where there might be rich gold, is obviously very deep, at least I haven't reached it yet." Bob mentioned.

It was a timbered hole of about four feet in diameter, and above it stood a windlass, used to wind up buckets of dirt from the bottom of the hole.

"How could you work the windlass unless you had

someone else to help you?" asked Dan.

"Well I could work alone while the hole was shallow, but now that I am down about forty feet, I have to climb up and down the ladder with the buckets of dirt."

"Very slow going." commented Dan. "Why haven't you got some partners to help you?"

I have been here for only two seasons, and I wanted to see if the ground was rich enough to form a company, before I spent any more money." said Bob as he started down the shaft.

Carrying the second ladder with him, he placed it below the first one, so that it reached the bottom of the shaft.

"Turn the rope on the windlass, Dan, and send the bucket down to me." Bob called

As Bob shoveled a bucket full of dirt, and signaled to Dan to wind it up, Dan called down the shaft:

How do we separate the gold from the dirt?

"Oh, I forgot, you don't even know how to use a gold pan, do you?" asked Bob.

"Never had the opportunity" replied Dan, "but I'm willing to learn."

"Just wait there, I'll be right up" Bob called.

"I got to thinking, Dan," said Bob as he emerged from the shaft. "We could work a lot faster if you did the digging down there, while I pan out the dirt in the creek."

"Let's go down to the creek," suggested Dan, "I want to see how you operate a gold pan."

Standing in the shallows of the creek, Bob knelt down on a flat rock, holding the pan with both hands.

Immersing it under the water, and swishing it in a circular motion, he continued to remove the largest rocks in the pan until only sand and a thin line of black sand remained. Dipping the front of the pan in and out of the water, he eliminated the sand, leaving only the black sand, wherein three specks of gold were revealed.

"Well, not much there so far. We've got to get down to the bedrock." said Bob in an exasperated tone.

'He seems so optimistic, so sure' said Dan to himself' 'that he is going to find a deposit of gold, to me it is such a gamble.'

Back again at the shaft, it was now past midday, and both Bob and Dan were hungry. As they sat on the rocks eating hunks of bread and cheese, the dog Curly, smelling the food, put his paw up on Dan's lap.

"Awe come on Curly, you can wait until dinner time, don't bother Dan." With that the dog obediently removed his paw, whined a little, and then lay down.

As they finished their lunch, it was now Dan's turn to be down in the shaft.

While climbing down the ladders he kept thinking of a story he had read, of a miner who was left to die down in a mine shaft.

'But that could not happen here, not with the ladders in place.' said Dan to himself.

Down in the bottom of the shaft the coal oil lantern fastened to the ladder was still giving off a faint glow of light against the multi coloured rocks and stones in the walls. White quartz, green Country rock, pink quartz, and blue slate.

'Beautiful, really' thought Dan, 'but there's no sign of gold.'

It was about a week later as Dan was hard at work in the shaft, that his shovel hit on hard rock. Moving across to the other side of the hole, he struck the shovel down hard again. It also went into hard rock. Had they reached bedrock? Dan called up the shaft to Bob.

"Come down here Bob, are you there?" There was no answer, for only the dog Curly came over to the edge of the shaft and whimpered.

'He must be down at the creek' said Dan to himself.

"Hi Curly" called Dan. The dog wagged his tail and whimpered again. Just then Bob's head appeared.

"Hey Bob, come down here, I want you to see this."

"What is it Dan?" he called in an excited tone as he quickly made his way down the ladders.

"Have we struck gold?"

Dan showed Bob what he had dug up, and together they shoveled and picked, and dug all around the bottom of the shaft hole. They found nothing but large quartz bolders.

"Have the pans of dirt shown any increase in gold?"

"No, no more than the usual few flakes, but I have found one small nugget" he said, as he dug into his pocket. It was a pretty nugget of green gold, smooth sided, and about the size of a small toe nail.

"Perhaps we should keep digging around the rocks, or even under them, if we can get down that far." suggested Dan.

"I am sure this is bedrock" said Bob, "I think we have a dry hole here, and I can't afford to sink another shaft." Bob's face showed his disappointment and shock, so much so that Dan thought he might start crying.

"Don't be too sad, Bob," said Dan, putting his arm across his shoulder, "It's not the end of the world, after all, it was a gamble, but you are right, we should keep on digging for at least another few feet, just to be sure."

Try as they did, their efforts were fruitless.

"Are you sure you don't want to try again in another location on the claim?" inquired Dan.

"No, no, I am already in debt. Perhaps I could sell the claim to pay off my bills."

There was no gold, only white quartz boulders.

"Anyway, replied Bob, we'll have to move off this property and look for jobs"

"Well, first let's look for a boarding house, then at least we'll have a roof over our heads."

"The cheapest boarding house in town that I know of, is Alex McIinnis's, down in Cameronton," Bob told Dan, "I think they charge $6.00 a week."

"But we will still have to find work immediately, perhaps in one of the mines." added Dan. "I can pay for the first week's board"

Over the next week Dan helped Bob pack up his belongings in preparation for the move to town.

"We'll go and see my friend Joe Plaskett who has a shed behind his house on the back street. He might let me store my things there, at least for a while, until I figure out what to do next".

On their way to town to make arrangements for storage, they were met by several groups of miners returning from the south where they had spent the past winter.

"Will ye give us a ride down the hill?" they called.

"Jump aboard" called Bob.

"Those are the men of the Welsh Co. mine" he explained to Dan, "they are on their way to their claims at Caernarvon, up on Lowhee Mountain." As Dan looked back at the men climbing up on to the wagon, his heart fell, for there amongst them was Owen Parry, the man who had assaulted him on the barge the year before As much as Dan tried not to notice him, the offending Welshman spotted Dan and called out

"Ho ho, look what we have here, the young and tender boy from the other end of the country, although I must say he is a fiesty one."

The other men heard the comment, but did not understand the significance. From the way his companions treated him, it would appear that Owen Parry had gained some respect and promotion since Dan had last seen him.

On driving through "Middletown" where the miner Billy Barker had made a spectacularly rich strike of gold the summer before, they arrived at the community known as "Cameronton."

This part of the town had been named after the miner John Angus (Cariboo) Cameron, who also struck a rich vein of gold below the canyon on Williams Creek, in the winter of 1862, a few months after William Barker.

Bob drew the wagon up outside a two story log house.

"This is McInnis's boarding house" said Bob as he got down off the wagon and tied the reins to the hitching post. Dan followed him up a set of wooden stairs to a landing.

Knocking on the door several times, Bob had almost given up, when it was opened by a pretty young woman.

She looked to be quite exasperated and in a flustered mood, her curly black hair was in disarray and her face all red. In the background the sounds of an unhappy baby filled the air.

"Yes" she asked in a thick Scottish brogue, "What do you want?"

"Sorry to bother you ma'am, but we were looking for a place to board."

"Could you come back in an hour or two, I am trying to cook up a dinner here, and I am all by myself."

"Could we give you a hand?" put in Dan as he peered around the door. "I have had some experience in cooking." The room was obviously a kitchen, but the smoke was so thick he could hardly see to the other end.

"That is very nice of you" the lady replied, "for as you can see, I have my hands full, what with a dozen men to cook for, and a six months old baby to care for. Please leave the door open to let some of this smoke out. I have just burned the pies in the oven, oh dear." and with that she sat down in a chair and burst into tears.

Dan patted her on the shoulder and handed her a small dishtowel to dry her tears.

"How can we help? tell us what to do." he asked

"Well, if you really mean to help, you and your friend could peel those turnips there in that bucket, and put them on to cook. I also need some more wood for the stove. You will find a pile by the back door." I must see to the baby." she said through her tears, and with that she disappeared from the room.

"Looks like we arrived at just the right moment", said Dan.

"I'll bring some wood up, if you start on the turnips", suggested Bob.

It was not long before Dan and Bob had things under control, and the young woman returned with a baby in her arms.

"This is wee John" she told them, "he has started to get his teeth, and is in pain a lot. I am eternally grateful for your help, I could not have done without you."

Just then a young, tall, red headed man came through the back door. He also spoke with a thick brogue.

"Is dinner ready yet, my dearie?" he asked.

"Yes, almost, "A.D.", but it would not be, if it weren't for the help of these two young men. This is my husband Alexander McInnis" his wife replied, as she introduced Dan and Bob.

"We have come looking for a boarding place, Sir" spoke up Dan,

"We have to find work too" chimed in Bob.

"Stay and have dinner with us, if you wish, but I am afraid you cannot board here. I am a shareholder in the 'Cameron' claim here on Williams Creek, and we board only the men who work on the claim. At the moment we have more than enough men, but you could try at the Welsh Company, up at Caernarvon. I hear they are short of men."

This was not good news to Dan, for he did not want to see any more of Owen Parry.

At dinner that day Dan and Bob sat at a long table with a dozen Scottish men, including their leader, John A. Cameron. While the conversation was mostly about working their gold mine, it also touched on an impending court case involving Mrs. McInnis.

Apparently Elizabeth Roddy, which was her maiden name, had been engaged to a Joe Carruthers, the owner of a valuable mining claim. Upon their engagement, Carruthers had given Miss Roddy a share in his mine. When Miss Roddy broke her engagement and married McInnis, Carruthers sued Mrs. McInnis for the return of the mining share. The case was to come up before Judge Begbie that fall.

Following a very satisfying meal Dan and Bob said their good-byes and took their leave.

As they drove along the crowded street Dan noticed a young boy selling newspapers from door to door.

"Does this town publish a newspaper?" he asked Bob.

"Yes it does, it's called the Cariboo Sentinel. Why do you ask? Are you thinking of advertising for a job?

"No, I am wondering if I could get a job there. I am not half bad at writing."

"That's a good idea, it's worth a try" answered Bob, pulling the team up in front of the newspaper office.

"Don't bother waiting here for me Bob," called Dan as he jumped off the wagon, "meet me in the Wake Up Jake in a half an hour.

As Dan entered the door of the newspaper office he smelled the strong odor of printer's ink, and heard the loud sound of a press working, turning out two double sheets of printed matter, one at a time.

Working the press was a short, rather stout man in

his thirties, his printer's apron smeared with ink, and his pudgy, florid face covered in sweat.

Dan waited patiently until the man paused to put more newsprint in to the machine.

"Excuse me Sir" he began, "I was wondering if you need any help with your newspaper. I have traveled all the way from Newfoundland to reach the gold fields, and I need a job."

"All the way from back east eh? you don't look old enough to leave home, let alone travel clear across the country. Which group of 'Overlanders did you travel with? I am also an overlander, from Huntington, in Upper Canada." blurted out George Wallace in his excitement.

"Getting back to your inquiry lad, do you have any references? How much schooling have you had? Can you write a proper sentence?" asked Mr. Wallace.

"Yes, I have a reference from Mr. Boyd at Cottonwood. Didn't go to school much, Sir, but writing is my passion. I can show you, if you like."

"Write me a sentence about your home on this piece of paper." requested the editor, handing Dan a pencil and a sheet of paper.

Dan thought about it for a moment before he wrote in his careful, tidy hand "My home is a long, long way from here. It is a land beside the ocean, where fishing is the only subject of conversation."

"Very good" said the editor. "What is your name? Would you be willing to go out looking for news, would you consider being a reporter? You would have to write up the stories for me."

"Yes," replied Dan, "and I think I would enjoy it. How much would you pay me?"

"Never mind enjoying it, it's damned hard work, if you work for me. It would be seven days a week, from eight to eight. I could only afford to pay you $50.00 a month to start with. Maybe more later, if you stay on. There is a cot in the back of the room here that you can sleep on, but you will have to buy your own food. How would that suit you?"

"You've got a deal there" said Dan putting out his hand to shake, but drawing it back quickly when he saw the man's ink and grease smeared hands.

"My name is Dan McDermott, from Carbonear, Newfoundland, and your name Sir?"

"George Wallace. I own the newspaper; started it last year when I came up from Victoria. I bought the press from Armour De Cosmos, who started the Victoria Colonist. With the largest gold rush going on in British Columbia, I thought there should be a newspaper here."

"When do you want me to start, Sir?"

Right now, and you can drop the Sir bit, just call me George." mentioned the editor.

"I have to let my mate know that I have found a job, Sir, I mean George, I could be back in an hour or less." said an elated Dan.

"Alright, but get back here as soon as you can."

"Yes Sir, I mean George." answered Dan as he flew out of the door.

102

CHAPTER 7

The Young Reporter

It was a happy and exhilarated young man that met Bob in Andrew Kelly's coffee house shortly after.

"Good for you," Dan," said Bob when Dan told him of his good fortune. "I am sure you will do well there; it's what you like doing, anyway, much more so than working in a mine."

"What about you, Bob, have you thought about what you might do?" asked Dan.

"I think I will see if the Welshmen will take me on at their mine," he said

"If you are hired, watch out for that one known as Owen Parry, Bob, there is something queer about him; I would not trust him at all," advised Dan.

"I understand he is one of the owners of the Welsh Company," mentioned Bob.

"Is that so," said Dan, in a rather surprised tone, "I wonder how he got into that position. Anyway, I must get back to the newspaper, but keep in touch, eh? Drop in when you can, and I will do the same," Dan promised as he took his leave.

Back at the 'Sentinel' office, Dan was immediately put to work cleaning the 'Chase', which was the frame that held all the letters used in printing the paper. It was a messy job, and before he started George Wal-

103

lace made him put on a 'printer's' apron, to protect his clothing.

Once the latest edition was printed, Dan supervised three young boys who had been hired to distribute the paper.

In a plan he laid out, the area of the town was divided up into three sections; upper, which included the Marysville hospital on the east side of Williams Creek; middle, the area of Cameronton, and Barkerville, as far as Grouse Creek, and south, to Richfield.

One evening a few days later, Dan met Bob after work, and together they went into the Kelly Hotel for a beer.

"So, tell me Bob, did you get a job up at the Welsh Company's mine?"

"Yes, I did, I am working the graveyard shift, from midnight to noon." I started last Wednesday night; and I am working with a David Price, another Welshman. He is teaching me the ropes. It's only a six hour shift, but I get $6.00 a shift, and that's not bad."

"Not bad you say, I am only getting $50. a month!" exclaimed Dan.

"But then you are doing what you enjoy, whereas mine is only a job" mentioned Bob.

"Have you come across Owen Parry yet?" asked Dan

"Oh yes, as I have told you, he is one of the mine owners." said Bob assuredly.

"How many owners are there?" inquired Dan.

"Three, including Owen, Richard Evans, and Beavan Jones, all Welshmen."

Having finished their beers, the two friends left the hotel looking for some entertainment.

The loud music coming from James Loring's "Terpsychorean Saloon" down the street, lured them in, where they watched a performance of the Hurdy Gurdy girls and their partners.

Although termed as 'dancing', the action was more like an athletic exercise. The girls themselves were very young, some only in their early teens, while their male partners were older, and very muscular.

As the girls cavorted around in their scanty costumes, at certain stages they were thrown up into the air and caught by the men, who then released them to continue the performance. This sort of behaviour for decent women to indulge in was almost unheard of, and consequently the audience was all men.

One of these girls, a tiny, dark haired beauty, caught Dan's eye as she moved around the saloon. Dan became quite smitten with her; the way she danced, and her general manner and good looks made his heart beat faster. This was the first time he had ever felt this way about a girl.

"I must find out what her name is," he whispered to Bob.

"I understand the dancers are very closely guarded, and not allowed to fraternize with the public." mentioned Bob.

"Who looks after these girls?" Dan asked, "someone must sponsor them, for most of them are very young."

"I have heard that a lady known as Fanny Bendixon supervises them", said Bob.

Fanny Bendixon was an elegant, dark haired beauty from San Francisco who owned property and several saloons on Williams Creek during the early gold rush.

It is said that Fanny escorted the bevy of young dancers from San Francisco to the gold fields each summer, in order to fulfill a contract with a certain saloon keeper.

Following the performance Dan attempted to go into the back rooms of the saloon, to look for Fanny.

"Fanny is not here tonight", James Loring told Dan," you might catch her in her own saloon up the street, the "Parlour Saloon", next to Moses' barber shop." As Dan hurried along the street he was jostled by throngs of miners walking in groups, singing and enjoying themselves after a hard day's work in the mines.

On entering the "Parlour" saloon Dan looked around the noisy, smoke filled room, and spotted what looked to him to be the proprietor, Fanny Bendixon, standing at the bar, her bejeweled and elegant satin gown flowing around her.

"Excuse me 'Ma'am, are you Miss Bendixon?" ventured Dan.

"Yes", she answered, "and who wants to know?"

"Excuse me "said Dan as he told her,

"I understand you sponsor the dancing girls down at Loring's saloon."

"Yes" the lady replied, her attention drawn to one of her customers, who had ordered a drink.

"I am curious to know the name of one of one of the girls, the little young one with the dark hair, and the dimples."

"Oh yes, you mean Collette Dumais. Actually, she is not from San Francisco, her mother lives here near Richfield. Collette is a very gifted dancer, grew up in Victoria, you know. Her father died last fall, and her mother is destitute, so I gave her a job dancing with the German girls this summer."

"Can you tell me where she lives, I would like to visit her." asked Dan.

"I really can't give out that information" said Fanny, "I have to protect the girls from too much fraternization with the public."

Is that part of their contract?" asked Dan.

"Actually, not in the case of Collette. Tell you what, why don't you go to the back door of the Terpsycorean Saloon and wait for her to come out after they are finished, at shortly after eleven o'clock."

"Oh thank you so much for the information", said Dan. "Perhaps I can do you a favour some time?"

"I will remember that" said Fanny as she poured herself another drink and lit up a cigarillo.

Back at Loring's saloon, Dan found Bob and told him what he had found out.

"You're a fast worker." Bob remarked.

As the dancers moved off the saloon floor shortly after eleven o'clock, Dan said goodbye to Bob and quickly made his way to the back door of the building.

The girls were just coming out as he arrived, travelling together in a group, down the street, to their accommodations at Miss Bendixon's boarding house, that is, all but Collette. As he stood there, Dan seemed to be the only person waiting at the door.

A few minutes later the last of the dancers, Collette, emerged from the door and ran down the steps, but just as Dan was about to approach her, a figure came out of the shadows, and took Collette's hand. It was Owen Parry, the despised Welshman!

"How are you this evening my dear?" Dan heard him ask her.

Unabashed, Dan stepped forward, and taking the young ladies' other hand, he kissed it and said

"Good evening, Miss Dumais, I have been wanting to meet you. Your dancing was enchanting. You must have been dancing all your life."

Owen Parry was quite taken back by Dan's intrusion, but quickly recovered, and taking Collette by the arm, he led her off.

"You don't want to bother with the young waif from Newfoundland, now do you?" he remarked, in tones loud enough for Dan to hear.

Dan was annoyed at first, and disappointed, especially since it was Owen Parry who had interfered with his plans.

'Not to worry' said Dan to himself 'I will find out where she lives, and try again, to meet her.'

The next morning as Dan got back to the office from

eating breakfast with Bob, he found George Wallace hard at work on some articles he had prepared on the status of the mining claims in the outlying districts.

"I have a special assignment for you, Dan; and I want you to get started on it right away. I hear that William Luce, the miner and roadhouse keeper has arrived in town from Yanks Peak, on Snowshoe Mountain. Apparently the snow is still four feet deep up there, so it took him and the expressman Spooner, quite some time to reach Williams Creek.

I want you to interview him, his reasons for coming to Williams Creek, and any stories or anecdotes he might have to tell."

Where could I find him?" asked Dan.

"Possibly at Janet Allen's hotel in Cameronton." replied George.

With his notepad and pencil in hand, Dan grabbed his coat and hat, and hurried up the street.

Looking up at the sky, he could see that it was shaping up to be a very dull day, with a blustery wind blowing from the north. It felt more like winter than a day in June.

As he entered the Pioneer Hotel, a large, single story, frame structure, he came across the proprietor, Janet Allen, standing behind the front desk. A rather large, but affable lady, she told Dan that William Luce was registered at her hotel, but that he was so exhausted from his long journey, that he was not up yet.

"Come back in a couple of hours," she advised, "When I see him, I'll tell him to expect you."

As Dan made his way back, the traffic on the single, muddy, street was already picking up, ox carts and horse drawn wagons filled with various commodities, their drivers shouting to the pedestrians to get out of the way.

Suddenly, out of the corner of his eye, Dan spotted young Collette Dumais, accompanied by an older woman, gazing in at the window of the nearby Mason and Daly's store. Jostling his way through the traffic, Dan climbed up off the street to the raised sidewalk.

"Good morning Miss Dumais, how are you today? well I hope." said Dan, bowing. Turning her attention to him, Collette smiled and held out her hand.

"This is my mother," she said, introducing her companion, an older but very well groomed lady.

"What did you say your name was? I think you did mention it, but in the confusion of the moment, I have forgotten it."

As Dan introduced himself, Collette continued,

"I am so sorry about the other night, I rather think you took Mr. Parry by surprise.

"He took me by surprise, I did not see him, he was standing in the shadows."

"Perhaps you would like to come to our house to visit us", Collette suggested, "we live up on the hill above Richfield. You will know the house by the French flag flying outside." said Collette.

'Of course', said Dan to himself, 'I might have guessed that she was French, from her name.'

Just then Collette's mother broke into the conversa-

110

tion.

"I must remind you Collette, that you are engaged to Mr. Parry now, and he might not like you entertaining another man. Yes, Dan," she went on, "Collette is going to marry a rich mine owner."

Dan had neglected to notice the diamond ring on Collette's finger.

"No mother, I will see whom ever I want," said Collette very firmly. At the same time Dan detected a look of anguish and desperation on her lovely face.

"You wouldn't be doing this if your dear father was still with us" her mother whined.

"If father was still with us, you wouldn't be destitute." whispered Collette, when she suddenly became aware that passers by were listening to the loud conversation.

"My mother wants me to marry a rich man" Colleen whispered to Dan, as he started to back away, "and that's why she wants me to marry Owen Parry."

Dan was really taken back by all this, for he had not expected to be confronted with such a private conversation in such a public place.

'Is this how the French behave?' he wondered, as he said goodbye.

Later that day Dan returned to the Pioneer Hotel to look for William Luce the miner from Yanks Peak. He found him sitting in the lobby.

'Now here is a real character' Dan told himself as he shook hands with the man, 'this is going to be a story worth telling.'

Luce was a fairly tall and slim man, with an unruly head of ebony black hair. He also wore a mustache, which like his hair, was very much in need of attention. His gaunt face was typical of a man who had been used to going without luxuries, but whose countenance spoke of his love of life, no matter how rugged.

"What can I do for you, young man?" Luce asked, with a twinkle in his snapping black eyes.

"I am a reporter from the Cariboo Sentinel newspaper, and I would like to interview you" replied Dan

"That would be fine" said Luce, "but let's go into the saloon next door, and I will treat you to a beer."

"Thank you" replied Dan, but I don't drink liquor when I'm working, but I could use a sarsaparilla."

Seated in the almost empty saloon William Luce related a fascinating story to Dan, concerning his life on the slopes of Snowshoe Mountain, where he mined, and operated a roadhouse for passing miners and tradesmen.

"Wall", he began, "I had to make this trip to Willams Creek to register ma claims with the Gold Commissioner. Been meaning to come since last fall, but now that spring has come, I figured it might be safe to make the trip."

"To begin with, I came out here frem the Californee gold rush in 1859. Originally, I was frem Kentucky.

I have a partner, or I should say, I had a partner, Thomas Haywood, an Englishman. We built a cabin beside the creek up there, and worked together for quite a few years, until we quarreled about where to dig. So then we split up. I kept the cabin, and have lots of prospectin men stayin overnight with me."

"To entertain 'em I tell them bear stories, 'specially the one about shattering my Kentucky rifle. The one they likes the best though, is the story 'bout the mules that was caught in a snowstorm on the mountain,

That was last fall, when there was a sudden storm between Yank's Peak and Keithley, and a train of twenty mules was lost, buried in the deep snow.

It was after the storm were over, when two of my mates and I ventured out on snow shoes. Yu see we was on our way for supplies from the store at Keithley.

Suddenly we came across a mule's foot, stickin straight up, out of the snow. We dug down deeper, and found more mules, lying, still in their harness, and dead as doornails. There was no sign of any people. They must have high tailed it outta there when they could.

Up on the mountain, we are always short of meat, so, not wanting to waste any, we went back to the cabin and rounded up several sleighs, some sharp knives, a hand saw, and a couple of axes.

When we got back to the mules, we could see that we were going to have to fight for the meat, as there were four big black wolves there who had also discovered the meat, and were chewin on it with a vengeance. When we come along they growled and charged at us, and one of them sprang at me, its large teeth bitin at my face and arms. Lucky fer us we had our rifles with us, and Tom had to shoot the one that was bitin on me. This made the other three wolves back off."

"While two of my friends kept the wolves at bay, the rest of us got quite a lot of meat cut up and loaded on to the sleighs. We also took most of the leather and harness off the mules. By this time the wolves were getting very fierce again, so we stopped, and let them have the remains. The wolves, and later the coyotes, cleaned the meat all up, and now there is not a sign that the mules were ever there."

"That is a pretty scary story, Sir," said Dan as he finished writing his notes, "it will make a good article for the paper. Do you have any other stories, Sir?"

Oh yes, there's the one about the old peddler." replied Luce.

"An old what, did you say Sir?" asked Dan

"A Jewish peddler, who was also caught in a storm over the Snowshoe plateau." said Luce.

"He had been sellin small items to the miners in the gold camps all summer, things like combs, scissors, writing paper and ink, and oh yes, little round hand mirrors, from a supply he kept in a satchel he hefted over his shoulder.

It was late fall, and the days were growin cold as the old man started south on his journey over the mountain. Noticing the grey sky, and the dark, rollin clouds, the fore warning of a storm, he hurried on as best he could."

"He was very brave to be out there all by himself", commented Dan.

Dan interviews the miner, William Luce.

"He had just passed the shelter of a forest of Spruce trees, and as he walked out on to an open meadow, a sudden blizzard hit with such force that he was blinded, and just plum lost his way. A friendly Spruce tree, its branches extending down to the ground, provided the only shelter, and there the old man spent the night.

"Brrrrr", put in Dan, "He must have nearly perished."

By morning the storm had blown over, leaving at least two feet of fresh snow. As the peddler started out from under the tree, he floundered along through the snow, his pack of wares still upon his back, cold, lost, and hungry.

Just at this time I happened to be out on snowshoes, checkin my traps, when I came upon the old man. I helped him get through the snow by making hard tracks with my snowshoes, and got him back to my cabin. This had been a verra exhausting experience, and it was two days before the old man seemed to be himself agin. As he left my cabin and said goodbye, he reached into his pack, and pulled out a dozen little round mirrors, the size of an American dolla, and left them for me, in return for savin him, and for my kindness."

"Wow, that was interesting," exclaimed Dan, as he made notes. "What did you do with the little round mirrors?"

"I gave them away to anyone who wanted them. I haven't seen any lately."

"When do you expect to be going back home again, Sir?" asked Dan as he put his notes away.

116

"Just as soon as I can get my mule loaded up with supplies. I have to get back to my mine, now that spring is here."

"You mean, because the snow is melting, and the weather is warmer?" asked Dan.

"Yes that, but mostly because someone could be poachin on my ground." answered Luce.

Back at the newspaper office Dan found the Editor George Wallace in a great state of excitement.

"While you were gone, Dan, your friend Bob Chase came in to see you. He tells me that one of the partners of the Welsh Co. Mine has been missing for the last day, and no one knows his whereabouts."

"I got some great stories from Luce, sir, but I can leave that if you want me to follow up on this latest rumour" suggested Dan.

"No, no, I think you had better write up the Luce stories first, and then you can find Bob, to hear more about the disappearance."

"Which partner went missing? do you know?" asked Dan.

"No, Bob didn't say."

CHAPTER 8

The Missing Mine Owner

It was getting quite late when Dan finished writing up his interview with Luce. He had quite enjoyed doing it. It had been an exciting assignment, and one that he would like to follow up on.

'Perhaps some day I could ride over to see Luce at his mine.' said Dan to himself.

Just as he turned from talking with George, a young Chinese boy came through the door. He looked at Dan and asked

"You Mr. Dan?"

"Yes I am Daniel McDermott. Why do you ask?"

"My name Martin Chung, I hear you like to have some washing done? My father, Kwong Chung have bath house and laundly, velly good laundly. You like to have shirts washed and ironed?"

"Yes, I certainly do need to have some clothes washed. How much do you charge?"

"Fifty cents for large bundle." the boy answered.

"I will go and get you a bundle right now, wait here" said Dan.

"Will you bring the clothes back when they are ready?" asked Dan as he fastened up a big bundle of dirty clothes. "I would like them back soon, as I am almost out of clean clothes. What did you say your

118

name was?"

"Martin, yes, I bring back soon." he replied as he picked up the bundle and disappeared down the street.

The boy could not have been more than twelve or thirteen, but seemed to have learned a lot of English in his young life.

"Martin is the son of Kwai Chung, the Chinese merchant who has a bath house and laundry up the street" said George. "He brought Martin over from China six years ago, when he went back to visit his wife."

That evening as Dan arrived at the 'Wake Up Jake' restaurant, he looked around for his friend Bob, who had arrived before him.

"What's this I hear about a missing mine owner? who is it?" Dan asked.

"Richard Evans, the one with the limpy leg. His wife is terribly worried." disclosed Bob.

"Why, I remember seeing him limping down the street, when was it? yesterday? How long has he been missing?" asked Dan.

"Disappeared last evening, never came home last night, his wife says."

"I suppose the policeman, what is his name? is investigating?"

"Yes, Henry Fitzgerald, but with no success."

"Are they sure he didn't go to Quesnelemouth on the stage?" asked Dan.

"His wife would know, wouldn't she?" replied Bob.

"Well, you would think so, but then," said Dan as

Bob cut him short.

"His wife says she is sure he would not have gone anywhere; as they were going to celebrate a wedding anniversary today."

"Oh." said Dan "He's not a drinker, is he? I thought perhaps he might have been doing some early celebrating." he suggested. "I will go to see his wife in the morning, it will make a good headline for the paper."

"Yes, I can just see it now" said Bob gesturing with his arms outstretched

'LOCAL MINE OWNER MISSING.'

When Dan met with George Wallace the next morning, he suggested that he should interview Mrs. Evans over the disappearance of her husband.

"Yes, I know you are itching to persue the story of the missing man, and I do want you to do it, but first, I want you to finish interviewing the miners. You have not yet interviewed Henry Davis, the Welsh miner who is becoming known as 'Twelve Foot Davis', and also, I have thought of another Welsh miner that you should interview, Harry Jones, one of Captain Evan's men, and then of course there's Richard Willoughby, on Lowhee."

'God grief', thought Dan, 'will it never end?'

Setting out that very afternoon, Dan climbed up the trail toward Richfield to find Henry Davis.

As he proceeded he had to pick his way through piles of tailings, pieces of lumber, and across open ditches, left there by the miners as they went about their work. The woods virtually rang with the constant sound of hammering, boards being moved and dropped, and the sound of men calling back and forth to each other.

In Williams Creek itself, a series of various sized wooden water wheels screeched, groaned, and moaned, as they turned on their wooden axles. Above that was heard the constant sound of axes, chopping down the nearby trees to use as props in the tunnels, and to build the miner's cabins.

Henry Fuller Davis was a shoemaker by trade, but he was also anxious to make some money mining gold. Noticing that there was twelve feet of open ground between the Diller and Abbott claims, he staked it, and mined $12000 in gold from it, the first year.

The Davis' claim was just north of Richfield, but having never met Davis made it hard for Dan to find him.

Shortly before he reached Richfield Dan noticed three men working in a small area on the east side of Williams Creek, between two larger mines.

'I wonder if this is it?' he asked himself.

Battling his way across the creek, he managed to get close to a short, squat man, dressed in overalls, with a big, felt, slouch hat on his head.

"Excuse me, sir, I am looking for Henry Davis."

"Well, you have found him" said the man, who spoke with a strong Welsh accent.

"What is it you want, young man? Can't you see I'm very busy."

Dan explained the need for an interview, but the

man laughed.

"No time right now, Tadpole; but I will meet you tonight down at Joe Denny's Saloon, at eight o'clock. alright?"

"Thank you sir, yes that would be fine." replied Dan.

Since he could not do his interview right then, and still had several hours before dark, Dan decided he would throw caution to the winds, and go to see Mrs Evans on Caenarvon Ridge.

As he walked along Dan tried to think of all the possible reasons for the disappearance of the mine owner, but all he could think of were reasons why he should NOT have disappeared.

The mine was doing well, it was producing over a 1000 ounces of gold a week, and he had not heard of any discord amongst the three partners.

His friend Bob Chase was still working there, but said he did not have much to do with Owen Parry, although he understood that Parry and Jones were not as well liked as Richard Evans.

As Dan continued to climb the hill he passed by the Welsh Co. shaft house where a large Cornish water wheel was working, the creaking and screeching of its timbers so loud it could be heard for miles around. Around about he encountered a group of mine workers busy at their various jobs.

Up near the summit of the mountain he came across a number of log cabins occupied by the mine workers. They did not stand in a row, as on a street, but were scattered here and there, and all had small gardens. Although they were small, they were built of large logs, only six logs high, with shake roofs and only one window. Most had chimneys adapted from mining flume pipes, although the odd one had a chimney made from sticks and clay.

Above these were the homes of the three Welsh mine owners, Richard Evans, Beavan Jones, and Owen Parry. They all faced south with windows that looked across the valley to the community of Richfield.

The most complete and permanent looking house was that of Richard Evans. Built of logs like the others, it had dove tailed corners and several custom made windows and doors. 'But then' thought Dan, 'Evans is the only married man of the three partners.'

Although the Evans' did not have any children, it was said that his wife was very clever with her hands, and occupied herself with fancy baking, which she sold, and was even known to do some carpentry work about the house.

Knocking on the front door, Dan waited, and when there was no answer, he knocked again. This time a middle aged woman with an anxious expression on her face, opened the door. She was tall, handsome, and well built, and carried herself with an air of confidence.

"Mrs. Evans?" Dan began as she nodded her head in assent. "I am Dan McDermott, a reporter from the Cariboo Sentinel newspaper. I am very sorry to hear that your husband is missing. It is possible that an article in the paper could help to find him."

Thank you for coming" she said, in a strong Welsh accent, the end of each sentence rising in pitch, "come into the kitchen, and we'll talk."

The lady led the way, taking Dan into a cheerful room where a large iron cook stove dominated the scene, and where a black kettle simmered away.

"Can I make you a cup of tea? you've had a long walk to get here.

"Oh thank you" said Dan "it would be most welcome."

As she busied herself at the stove and got out two cups and a tin of biscuits, Dan detected a slight catch in her voice.

"How old are you Dan?" she asked, "you look so much like my younger brother I left behind in Wales."

"I am sixteen now," said Dan, "and I came from Newfoundland."

"To the goldrush, no doubt." she added.

"Looking for adventure mostly, I have already learned that gold mining is not as easy as you might suspect." mentioned Dan. "But to get on with your missing husband, Mrs. Evans, what age was he? Please give me a description of him."

"He is fifty five, six feet tall, with dark brown hair, like all Welshmen. The last time I saw him he was leaving to attend a meeting with the other miners at the Welsh Co. meeting hall in town. That was at about seven o'clock last night. They were to decide on which of the three owners would represent the company at a conference in Wales next year. I was hoping that if

Richard was chosen, I could go along and visit my people there."

"Well, we'll have to find him" said Dan in a conciliatory tone. "What do the other two partners have to say about this? Have you talked to them?"

"No" said Glynnis Evans "there hasn't been time. They will be at work until dark. I hope to see them then, if Richard is still missing."

As Dan and Mrs. Evans sat drinking tea and talking, Dan wondered if he should give the lady his opinion of Owen Parry. Of Beavan Jones he knew nothing, but he was sure there was something unsavory about Owen Parry.

'No,' he thought, 'it would not be professional of me to give a personal opinion in this instance.'.

There was one further question he wanted to ask.

"Was Mr. Evans coming straight home after the meeting? Would he not have come home with the others?

"If you are asking if they might have stopped off at a saloon after the meeting, I assure you, Mr. Evans does not drink."

"So, if the others did stop off, Mr. Evans would have walked home by himself." suggested Dan

"Many's the time he has done just that." replied Mrs. Evans.

Having finished his tea, Dan thanked Mrs. Evans and left the house with the excuse that he had to get back to the Sentinel office.

On the way down the mountain Dan noticed that

the Welsh Co. mine had shut down, and the workers had walked off.

Just then he spotted Bob Chase.

"What is going on? Why has the mine stopped working?"

"Mr. Jones and Mr. Parry have decided that all the men should stop work, to make a thorough search for Mr. Evans. The policeman, Mr. Fitzgerald is coming to conduct the search."

"That's a good idea" said Dan, "wish I could help, but I must get back to George and the paper."

Further downhill Dan met a crowd of men going uphill to the mine, led by the policeman who was in uniform. "Coming to help in the search Dan?" he called.

"Wish I could, but I must get back to town, Henry." Dan called back.

Down at the newspaper office, George Wallace was up to his elbows in printer's ink, preparing the edition for the next day.

Dan told George that he had found Henry Davis, but had been unable to interview him until later that evening. He also told him that he had talked with Mrs. Evans.

"I see your curiosity is getting the best of you, Dan, but then, you did get some valuable information."

"Well Dan, now that you have interviewed

Further down the hill Dan met a crowd of men

Mrs. Evans, sit down and write it up, the article is going on the front page of tomorrow's paper. Oh, and are there any clues as to the whereabouts of the missing man? No, well hurry up and get your article ready."

It was quite late when Dan went for supper at the 'Wake Up Jake'. He had to gulp down his food to get to Joe Denny's saloon, to keep his appointment with Henry Davis.

The saloon was crowded, and the cigar smoke so thick that Dan found it hard to breathe.

Looking around, he spotted Henry Davis sitting at a table across from the door. Surrounding him was a group of men, obviously his admirers, conning him for any free drinks that were offered.

"Ah," called Davis, when he saw Dan coming toward his table.

"Here comes the little tadpole I met this afternoon. Would you believe it boys, he wants to interview me." There was a loud guffaw from the crowd around him as Davis drew up a chair for Dan.

"What are you drinking? my little Tadpole," he asked.

"I am not your little tadpole, sir, and I don't drink liquor while I am working."

There was another guffaw from his companions at Dan's remarks, and Davis' wide grin changed to a scowl.

"Well, I don't give interviews to rude little tadpoles, so you can go home now." he told Dan.

At this Dan rose from his chair, and left the saloon.

When he reached the Sentinel office, Dan found that George had gone home, so he let himself in, and went to bed.

"I don't blame you for not putting up with Henry Davis," said George when he heard the results of the interview. "Davis is all puffed up from having found so much gold on his little fraction claim." said George, "but, as I told you when you first started, you have to overlook the insults. Think of the old nursery rhyme, "sticks and stones may hurt my bones, but words will never harm me."

It was nearly noon before Dan had his article on Mrs. Evans ready, and George his 'furniture' of advertisements, placed on the same page. The two men worked hard, and by two o'clock, the little boys of the town were out selling papers.

"You had better get yourself some dinner, Dan, you must be starved" said George Wallace. "You have worked hard. Why don't you come with me, and we'll go together to the 'Wake Up Jake" But before they could think of leaving the shop the two men had to use a lot of printer's oil and old rags to get the ink off their hands.

In the crowded restaurant they managed to get a table near the window, and were eventually served by a harried waiter.

"They never hire enough staff," he said as he apologized for the long wait. They both ordered 'Caribou Stew' from the menu, and as Dan looked around at the throng of people arriving and leaving, he spotted young Collette Dumais, the dancer, just leaving.

'She will be going to work now' thought Dan to himself. 'I must get up to visit her. She will think I have forgotten her.'

As they ate, George Wallace mentioned his future plans for the paper to Dan.

"It will not be long before the fall court assizes, when Judge Begbie comes to town. We will have to cover the cases, especially the Felker case. I don't see how they can find him guilty, but we shall see.

I also want to finish the series of articles on various miners of the district, like the one you did on Luce. There are quite a few others that I have thought of, such as Neamiah Smith, who mines in the canyon. By the way, I hear they call him 'Blackjack', and Ned Stout, who is mining up the mountain, near the Welsh Co. claims."

"I also want you to interview the miners in the Antler Creek area, Ranald McDonald, John Rose, and James May."

As they sat planning the future contents of the paper, Dan noticed Owen Parry through the window of the restaurant, walking down the street.

"If you will excuse me, George", said Dan, wiping his face with his napkin and rising up off his chair, "I must catch up to Owen Parry; I see him passing on the street there. I want to make an appointment to interview him and Beavan Jones as soon as possible. I will settle up with you over the meal later."

Dan half ran out of the restaurant, and along the raised sidewalks outside the shops. Despite the fact that it was evening, the muddy street was still very busy with horse and mule driven wagons and buggies, their drivers calling loudly, each one trying to outdo the others as they directed their animals along the single thoroughfare.

As Owen Parry ducked into the Hudson's Bay Co. store on the west side of the street, Dan darted between the traffic, jumping over the puddles, and got across the street to the steps leading up to the store. He met Owen Parry in the doorway.

"I have been meaning to talk to you about the disappearance of Richard Evans, Owen, could we meet somewhere to talk? I want to know when you saw him last.

"You are not the policeman, Dan, why should I answer to you? However, If you must know, it is my understanding that Richard Evans went straight home after Beavan Jones and I left him, following the meeting.

"Who was chosen to represent the company at the conference next year?" asked Dan?"

"None of your damn business. I can tell you have been talking to Mrs. Evans." replied Owen Parry indignantly.

"That's alright", said Dan, "I can find out from a friend of mine."

"Oh, you mean Bob Chase, yes, I've been meaning to fire him, he is much too mouthy." said Parry. "Oh, and by the way, I will thank you for not consorting with Miss Collette; you seem to forget that we are engaged to be married." he added as he brushed past Dan, and continued down the street, his walking cane sticking into the mud at every step.

'I guess I will have to have a talk with the policeman, Henry Fitzgerald to get his story' decided Dan.

It was too late that evening to see the policeman, but the next morning, after getting permission from George Wallace, Dan sought out Sergeant Henry Fitzgerald.

At the station on the back street he found the Sergeant gone, and in his place the 2nd policeman, Constable Eric McPherson, who was waiting for Fitzgerald to arrive at any minute. While he waited Dan asked the policeman about Evans.

"It seems very strange for him to have disappeared so suddenly" mentioned the constable, "it was only a couple of days ago when I saw him at the mine with Owen Parry."

When Sergeant Fitzgerald did arrive, he was in a dreadful hurry, with no time to stop and talk to Dan. Apparently he was on his way up to Tom Maloney's roadhouse, on Bald Mountain, where he expected to find and arrest the outlaw 'Liverpool Jack'. After he had gone, Dan asked the constable:

"Have you had any leads as to the disappearance of Richard Evans?"

"No, it's just as if he had vanished into thin air", he replied.

"The Sergeant said something about 'Liverpool

Jack'" mentioned Dan.

"Yes, he is alleged to have killed a man in a saloon last night, and is attempting to flee the country by the back trails."

"I have never come across that shady character" said Dan "I believe he is an Englishman of doubtful character."

"Yes," said the policeman, "he is a trouble maker of the first order. He is also a gambler, said to have arrived early in 1862 from California, where he has a long criminal record."

Just as they spoke, the door to the police station flew open, and in came a man wearing a clergymen's, garb, and a wide brimmed, black hat. He was all out of breath, and in a great state of excitement.

"I want to report the presence of an outlaw in Tom Maloney's roadhouse up on Bald Mountain." he exclaimed.

"Yes, thank you, Reverend Dundas, but we have already been told about that; Sergeant Fitzgerald has gone to arrest him."

"Well" said the parson, "I can tell you, that was a very scary experience. I was on my way up to Antler Creek, when I stopped in at Maloney's roadhouse for a rest, and a bite to eat.

I sat at a table where a rough looking individual was devouring his food as if it was the last morsel left on earth. I spoke to him, but he would not answer me, giving me only wild glares. Just then another rough looking individual entered the room, shouting 'Look out there' to the man sitting at my table."

At this the man rose up off his seat, and turned and flew like a shot, out of the back door of the house."

"A few minutes later Sergeant Fitzgerald arrived, inquiring as to the whereabouts of the outlaw, but of course by this time he had gone.

I was quite shaken up, I can tell you, to think that I had been sitting at the same table with a murderer."

"Here sit down, Sir, and calm yourself" said the constable to the Reverend Dundas, "I will get you a drink of water."

Back at the office of the Sentinel newspaper, Dan had a lot to report to the editor. Then he asked,

"Who is this Reverend Dundas? I have not seen him before."

"He is one of Bishop Hills clerics, I believe stationed at Antler Creek for the summer." George Wallace told Dan. "He was here to attend the funeral of the miner John Emmory, just recently.

"You could write a report of his experience up at Maloney's, meeting up with 'Liverpool Jack." suggested George.

"Yes, I could, but we don't seem to be getting anywhere with the disappearance of Richard Evans" mentioned Dan. "Even the constabulary seem to be too busy to investigate."

"I think we need a larger police force here." suggested George as he finished putting together an other article for the next edition of the paper.

It was almost dark that evening as Dan and George

Wallace were locking up, when young Martin Chung came to the door of the Sentinel office. He had been running and was all out of breath, but kept repeating,

"Must talk to Mr. Dan, I have message for him."

"Yes, what is it Martin?" asked Dan.

"Message is from Ah Foo at Cottonwood. He say Mr. Dan come quick, need help."

This news gave Dan quite a shock. Busy at the newspaper on Williams Creek, he had almost forgotten his friends at the Cottonwood farm

Thank you for the message, Martin. I will try to get there as soon as I can."

"I really can't spare you right now, Dan" George Wallace told him, "things are so busy, what with the missing mine manager, and the interviews I want you to do. However, I do realize that young Martin's message sounded very desperate. You could take the stage out tonight, to see what is going on, and hopefully return as soon as possible."

"Oh thank you sir" said Dan, "I don't think they would be calling for me if it wasn't very important."

"Perhaps not" agreed George Wallace.

The stage coach to Quesnelemouth was due to leave Williams Creek at seven that night, and Dan would be on it as far as the Cottonwood farm. He had just an hour to eat supper, and perhaps see Bob. Bob could let Collette know that he was leaving town.

Gathering up a few items of clothing in his pack, Dan walked into the 'Wake-Up-Jake' restaurant. Bob was there talking to the proprietor, Andrew Kelly.

"I have to go down to Cottonwood farm to see Ah Foo, the Chinese cook", he told Bob.

"I hope it's nothing serious" said Bob.

"I may be gone for a day or two. Will you please let Collette Dumais know?" asked Dan.

"Certainly" said Bob. "Keep away from Owen Parry" warned Dan, "he is a very jealous man"

As the stage pulled out of Williams Creek Dan sat back against the leather seats that he shared with several other passengers. Most of these were business men, (one was Moses, the Negro barber,) on their way south, perhaps as far as Quesnelemouth, from where they would take the sternwheeler to Soda Creek. South of that they would have to take another stage coach to Yale.

By the time the stage reached Beaver Pass House it was getting dark, and when it stopped to take on a passenger, the driver lit the two coal oil lamps which were fastened on to the sides of the coach. It was just past ten o'clock when they reached the Cottonwood farm.

Engulfed in darkness and without a moon to light his way, Dan got off the stage and walked in to the back door of the darkened roadhouse. He tapped lightly on the door, which was opened almost immediately by Ah Foo, carrying a lantern.

"Mr Dan, thank you for coming so quickly." he said.

"What is the problem, Foo?" asked Dan.

It's Ah Fat, he is dying, and he wants to see you

136

before it is too late.

What is it, is he ill? has there been an accident?" asked Dan.

"None of those" said Ah Foo, "he has been mortally wounded by robbers."

"It happened last night, just as Ah Fat was on his way to bed He heard an unusual sound in Mr. Boyd's study, where the safe is kept. When he went to investigate, three men attacked him with daggers."

"Were these whites, or Chinese men?" asked Dan.

"They were Chinese; all strangers to Ah Fat. He said the robbers were not from around here. They were all tall men, probably from Mongolia."

Leading the way with his lantern, Ah Foo took Dan along a corridor to Ah Fat's bedroom.

By this time John Boyd had joined them.

"Poor Ah Fat," he said, "he was very brave, to have scared off the robbers and saved the cash as he did. He didn't stand a chance against them, they had knives, and they stabbed Ah Fat several times." John explained. "They were about to open the safe when Ah Fat interrupted them. They fled from the house when they saw me."

Ah Foo quietly opened the door to Ah Fat's bedroom.

The old Chinese cook was lying on his back, his face, arms, and chest were bandaged so completely that barely a spot was open for him to see by.

"Mr. Dan, is that you?" the corpulent oriental asked, "I am so glad you came, I am going to die soon, but I had to see you first."

On hearing that Ah Fat wanted to be alone with Dan, Mr. Boyd and Ah Foo tiptoed out of the room.

Dan sat down on the edge of the bed and held one of Ah Fat's bandaged hands.

"What is it you want to tell me, old friend?"

The elderly Chinaman started to cough, and when Dan held a rag to his mouth, bright red blood spurted out.

"I want you to arrange for my daughter Gee, who is twelve years old, to come to British Columbia. My wife died a few months ago, and Gee is living with her grandmother in a little village in Tsingtao, a coastal port, north of Shanghai. The grandmother is very ill, and will not live long. I have enough money put away in a bank in Quesnelemouth to pay for the expenses. I have also written a letter in Chinese, authorizing you to be her sponsor. A lady friend in Quesnelemouth will look after Gee when she gets here. Please do this for me, or I cannot die in peace."

Dan was absolutely stunned when he heard this request.

"I would think that John Boyd would be more capable of doing this, than I would, Ah Fat." he said.

"No, no" whispered, Ah Fat "John Boyd would not approve."

"Have you asked him?" asked Dan.

"Yes, I have, and he refused. He said the girl would be better off left in China. But I know she would lead the life of a dog there. I must have her brought here, to

Canada."

The exertion of talking, combined with his extreme anxiety, caused Ah Fat to cough up more blood.

"I feel totally incapable of this task, Ah Fat," Dan told him, as he sopped up the blood, and settled Ah Fat back on the pillows, "but I will, with your permission, consult with John Boyd about carrying out your wishes."

"I cannot thank you enough, dear friend," whispered Ah Fat, "I knew I could count on you." "Here," he said, handing Dan a parcel wrapped in a flour sack, "this contains all the necessary items you will need to complete my request."

Just then Ah Fat looked as if he was going to start coughing again, so Dan gave him a drink of water, and settled him down again. As Dan left the room, the Chinaman seemed to be resting peacefully.

'He will sleep now; and I will check on him in the morning' Dan said to himself.

It was too late by this time, to speak with John Boyd; besides, Dan had to think over Ah Fat's request first.

On finding an empty bedroom along the hall, Dan undressed and climbed into bed. He began to think about the day's events, but within minutes he was fast asleep.

It was the singing of birds outside his window the next morning, that woke Dan up with a start.

Jumping out of bed he pulled on his trousers, and ran down the hall to Ah Fat's room. Opening the door, he peeked in. Ah Foo was there, asleep in a chair beside the bed.

Ah Fat was lying in the same position as Dan had left him the night before. Dan knew just to look at him, that he was dead. Touching his hand, it was stone cold. Ah Fat had probably died soon after Dan left him.

Without disturbing Ah Foo Dan retraced his steps down the hall, where he found John Boyd and his wife in the kitchen, starting a fire in the big cookstove, and preparing to make breakfast.

"Ah Fat is gone." announced Dan, "I suppose he will have a Chinese funeral."

"Yes, I am sure Ah Foo will make the arrangements with his fellow countrymen at their village." replied John Boyd.

"What do you think of Ah Fat's request that his daughter be brought over from China?" Dan asked John.

"I think it would entail a lot of work to arrange her immigration." replied John.

"I have promised Ah Fat that his wishes will be attended to, and although I have not the least idea of how to go about it, I intend to see that this is done." confided Dan.

"If you want me to, I will set the wheels in motion" said John, "I have some connections, but it may take months to get the girl over here."

"We can only try." replied Dan.

Mrs. Boyd had a large pot of coffee made by this time, and before long there was also a saucepan of steaming porridge.

"You will try to get word to me as to how the negotiations are going, Sir?" and if there is anything more I can do to help." asked Dan."

"I don't think you will be expected to attend Ah Fat's funeral", said Boyd, as he directed Dan to a seat at the breakfast table, "these Chinese have their own traditions."

"I must get back to Williams Creek as soon as I can", said Dan, "since there is nothing more I can do here."

"I have to make a trip to Williams Creek today, to attend to some business", mentioned Boyd, "you could come with me."

"That would be wonderful, thank you" answered Dan.

"Where are your daughters?" Dan asked Mrs. Boyd "are they not coming for breakfast?"

Actually, Dan was curious to see Agnes, the daughter who had an affair with Harry Morfitt some months back.

"Mary Ann is in Quesnelle Mouth visiting her fiance Alfred Carson," she replied, "and Agnes is at the coast, visiting with an Aunt, and having her teeth repaired. She will not be home for awhile. Only Ida and Alice are at home. It is time they came for breakfast."

'Agnes is seeing her dentist?' wondered Dan, "how long does it take to see your dentist?'

A few minutes later the two girls, Ida and Alice came into the kitchen.

"Hello there Dan," both girls said as they welcomed Dan. "I hear that you have a good job with the newspaper in Williams Creek," mentioned Alice, the older of the girls.

"Yes, it keeps me very busy, and in fact I should be getting back there right away." said Dan.

"Would you like to come out to the barn to see my new saddle horse, Dan?" asked little Ida.

"Yes, Ida, I hear that you are a very good rider. Your father and I will be out at the barn as soon as breakfast is over, we are leaving for Williams Creek."

Ida's much admired horse was a young, high strung gelding, bought by John Boyd from George Hyde of Beaver Pass.

Bidding the Boyd family farewell, John and Dan left in the buggy, and headed up Lightning Creek toward Richfield. It took only two hours and a half, with stops at Van Winkle, the roadhouse at Ground Hog Lake, and then Richfield.

On reaching town, John took the horse into Mundorf's stables to be fed and watered while he went about his business, and Dan hurried down to the Sentinel office, to let George know that he was back.

"That was a very short trip, I must say" commented George, "but I am glad you are back, I am just swamped with work."

Dan took John Boyd for lunch at the 'Wake Up Jake' restaurant as payment for his ride back to Williams Creek. While there Dan asked Andrew Kelly if any new developments had occurred in the mystery of the missing men, while he had been away.

"None that I have heard" replied Andrew."

When Dan went to see Sergeant Fitzgerald he received a thorough dressing down.

"Don't leave town again without telling me" he emphasized, "or I shall have to fine you."

As the Welsh Co. Cornish wheel stood quiet up on the mountain, the search for Richard Evans continued on for two days, with no tangible results.

'It is almost like a memorial to the missing man.' thought Dan as he walked toward the enormous Cornish water wheel, looking for the mine owner Beavan Jones.

"We do this when someone dies", remarked Gifford Parrish, one of the mine workers.

"It is too quiet, it's like a funeral," said another man as he passed Dan.

Dan found Beavan Jones in the shaft house, working on some accounts.

"I understand Richard Evans left you and Owen Parry after the meeting at the Cambrian Hall last week?" asked Dan. "Was that the last time you saw him?"

"Yes, it was. He said goodnight to us, and then headed off in the direction of his home on Caenarvon Ledge."

Beavan was a clean shaven man of about thirty, by far the youngest of the three mine owners. He was dark haired, and quite good looking, except for a deep scar on his right cheek.

"Got that scar as a youngster, when I fell on the sharp edge of a shovel." he explained.

"Have you been in the Cariboo for long, Beavan?" asked Dan, "what brought you out here?"

"I was sent out here from Cardiff by the investors of the mine in 1862. Inspite of what you hear, the mine is not making money, and may be closed down soon."

"Is any gold missing? is that why Richard Evans is missing?"

"Yes, actually quite a large quantity of gold is missing, that is why I have been going over the books. The records show that far more gold has been recovered, than has been shipped."

"I would thank you to keep these facts quiet for the time being, Dan, at least until we find Richard." mentioned Beavan.

CHAPTER 9

The Miners of Antler Creek

For the next few days Dan was kept busy helping George with the newspaper, but finally he had a spare evening.

'I must see how Bob is doing' he said to himself, 'I wonder if Owen Parry fired him. Actually he would have to have a pretty good reason to do so, not just because Bob is mouthy.'

As he entered the 'Wake Up Jake' to look for Bob, Dan could not see him anywhere, and concluded that perhaps he was still working. Just as he went back out of the door, he spotted Bob, down the street, headed his way.

"I was afraid you got fired" said Dan as Bob came up onto the sidewalk, "Owen Parry doesn't like you."

"Yes, I suspected that, and he did try to fire me, but the other partner, Beavan, overruled him, as I am the only one of the crew who knows how to turn the water off the wheel properly."

"Good for you, Bob, It sounds like you have an ally in Beavan. Have you heard anything more about Richard Evans?"

"His wife was down to the mine the other day, she had quite a talk with Beavan and Owen. I think she is going to ask the police to increase their investigation."

145

"The mine must be short of supervisors with Richard gone." said Dan.

"Yes, the other two are having to work extra long shifts, and although Beavan does not show it, Owen is very short tempered with the men."

'This would be a good time for me to visit Collette', thought Dan, Owen is probably too busy to be with her.'

It was late one evening as Dan stood outside the back door of James Loring's 'Terpsychorean' saloon, waiting for Collette. She seemed as always, to be the last of the dancers to leave.

This time he walked around the perimeter of the darkened yard, checking all the shadowy corners, to make sure Owen Parry was not lurking there.

Although it was a very dark fall night, it was still warm with a slight breeze blowing from the north that swept up the street in clouds of dust. From out of nowhere could be heard the sounds of a few stragglers meandering along the street, their figures illuminated by the lights in the buildings as they passed by. There was also the occasional clip clop sound of a horse and wagon returning from some distant place.

Suddenly the back door opened and out came Collette, lifting her skirts as she walked down the steps to the street. Looking around, she spotted Dan, who had stepped forward to meet her.

Good evening Collette," he said, as he smiled and took her hand.

"It is good to see you Dan" she replied "I was wondering when I would see you again."

"The newspaper has kept me very busy, especially since Richard Evans disappeared."

"Yes, isn't it terrible? I can't believe it, and also over that incident with Liverpool Jack. Did you write that article?"

Dan was flattered that Collette appreciated his writing, but did not answer her questions.

"I have come to walk you home, Collette, and to ask you some questions. Have you seen Owen Parry lately?" asked Dan.

"Not for almost a week now, he must be working longer hours." Collette replied.

"Have you had a chance to question him about the night Richard disappeared?" Dan asked. "Sometimes people mention little things that might provide a clue to the mystery."

"Well, let me see" said Collette, taking Dan's arm." Dan felt a warm tingle as she drew close, she was such a lovely little thing. Although her long dark hair was badly disheveled from a night of dancing, her clear, pink skin and dark red lips were almost irresistible.

"When I first asked Owen about the mystery, he laughed, and said that it was probably not a mystery at all, and that there had to be a logical solution. Owen also suggested that Richard might have left town on a horse, for some reason his wife did not know about." explained Collette.

"There's a good clue" said Dan, has anyone checked the livery stables? Does Richard own a horse?"

147

"It seems to me that he keeps one at Mundorf's stables, I remember seeing him riding one." commented Collette.

"But he didn't mention anything about leaving town to anyone, let alone his wife." declared Dan.

By now the two young people had walked quite a distance, and in fact were so intent in their discussion that they had not realized they had already reached the community of Richfield. As they passed by the last of the darkened buildings on the single street, they turned uphill to a graveyard.

"This is the Chinese graveyard" said Collette. "If we cut through it, my house is just on the upper side, in fact you can see it from here, the one with the French flag flying out in front."

"Oh yes, I see it" said Dan as he helped Collette over a style at the top end of the graveyard.

The house was a single story frame building, with a verandah across the front. In the window facing the front of the house a candle burned.

"My mother always leaves a lighted candle in the window if I am not home when she goes to bed." explained Collette.

As they drew close to the house Dan opened the garden gate for Collette, but stopped at the bottom of the stairs leading up to the verandah.

"It is so late, Collette, and we both have to work tomorrow, so I will leave you here. I was glad I caught you at the saloon, and that Owen was not waiting for you." whispered Dan.

"Yes, mon cheri" Collette whispered, "my mother is still worried that I am going to offend Owen by seeing you." As she said this, Collette squeezed Dan's hand. Dan was so moved by her obvious friendship, that he took her by the waist and gave her a big hug. It only lasted for a moment, and then he let her go.

"Au revoir, my dear" she called softly as she crossed the verandah, and entered the house. "I hope to see you again soon"

His hug, and the fact that she was not repulsed by it, told Dan that Collette welcomed his attentions.

'I cannot imagine her being happy married to Owen Parry' he told himself 'she could not possibly be in love with him. The idea of marriage must be her mother's influence.'

It was a warm evening a few days later when Dan noticed a cloud of dust appearing from behind the hill to the west of the town. Suddenly, as the dust cloud grew larger, a stage coach and four sturdy horses appeared driving fast, towards him

The coach was slowing down as the driver called to the horses and reigned them in. They snorted and whinnied to each other, knowing that now they would be able to rest, drink, and enjoy a feed of oats after their long journey.

As the coach came to a stop outside the Hotel de France, the driver got down from his seat, and opened the door. Four passengers alighted; Mr. Bill Blackmore of the Slough Creek mine, Mr. Charles Pin, a local merchant, Judge Begbie's clerk, Mr. Arthur Bushby, and Judge Matthew Begbie himself.

The judge looked tired and gaunt, his tall, thin frame slightly stooped over his cane, as he carried a satchel and walked with Bushby, into the hotel.

George Wallace was also watching the arrival of the coach

"You had better get out there and find Mrs. Evans, Dan, I understand she intends to speak with Judge Begbie."

Dan took off his apron and dried his freshly washed hands on a towel. Smoothing his hair, he put on his jacket, grabbed his notebook and pencil, and walked up to the hotel. Just inside the lobby he came across Mrs. Evans. She looked decidedly haggard since Dan had seen her last, worrying over the disappearance of her husband. On her head of greying black hair she wore a quaint little straw hat, out of which protruded two long, menacing hat pins

"Good evening Mrs. Evans" said Dan, "I hope you are not losing faith that your husband will be found."

"I must tell you that the police have confirmed that Richard could not have left Barkerville on the night he disappeared." she told Dan, "and that they are now suspecting foul play." she continued, as a tear rolled down her cheeks. "I must speak with Judge Begbie, he will see that a more thorough search is made."

"Thank you for giving me that information" said Dan "I am hoping to speak to the judge myself, I want to get the agenda of the Assize court session."

150

The fall assize court began at 10.00 a.m. the next morning, and was held in the Richfield courthouse.

The room was packed with curious onlookers who came to witness the trial of Henry Felker, accused of intent to kill, and also the trial of James Barry, a gambler, accused of murdering the miner Morgan Blessing.

Following the settlement of several small disputes between a number of local mining companies, the first trial began.

Henry Felker, his rather opulent figure dressed in a suit and waistcoat, was brought in by Sergeant Fitzgerald, and placed in the prisoner's docket. He looked thinner than Dan had remembered him, but was just as feisty as ever!

"Vot a lot of fuzz over zumthin zat neffer happened." he remarked to his jailer.

Mr. Walker, the lawyer representing Felker put his case forward, pointing out that Bibel, the deceased, had a reputation as a troublemaker and a lay about.

"Henry Felker did not deliberately kill Bibel, it was an accident, from which Bibel did not recover" announced the lawyer emphatically.

Following this, the lawyer for the Crown brought in several witnesses, the same ones who had sat drinking with Bibel and Felker that fateful night.

"I saw him put out his foot to trip Bibel," said one.

"I heard him swear in German, that he would kill Bibel" said another.

Dan watched as the stagecoach came to a stop.

The evidence began to look very damming to Dan, who was almost expecting a guilty verdict.

The jury, made up of twelve miners, deliberated for only half an hour, and then declared Henry Felker 'Not guilty'

The courtroom burst into an uproar as the case concluded, and Henry walked out a free man.

Aside from a few acquaintances who came up to congratulate him, Henry was quite alone as he stood on the courthouse steps, his coat tucked under his arm. None of his family had come to the trial, expecting that he would be convicted. The degrading experience had been terribly hard, on not only Henry, but his whole family, who had suffered for months, under the stigma of Henry's incarceration.

Dan managed to get a few comments from the elated Henry Felker as he left the courthouse,

"I go mining now," he said, "to hell mit the farming, I go mining, but not here, I go to the States."

After a short recess, the trial of James Barry began. Mr H. P. Walker, lawyer for the Crown opened the case for the prosecution by calling on Chief Constable for the Cariboo Henry Fitsgerald, to give his testimony concerning the case.

Fitzgerald claimed that he had been informed by Washington Delayney Moses, on the 25th of May, that he and Daniel McDermott, a stable boy from Cottonwood ranch, had found the murdered body of Morgan Blessing.

Fitzgerald and his deputy had witnessed the body

on the 27th of May, where it lay in a recess of ground, covered over with leaves and branches, about a mile east of Edward's Pine Grove House. Blessing had received two fatal stabs in the back and stomach region. Blessing's nugget pin had been recovered from the Hurdy Gurdy girl, and several other items from Blessing's pack had been confiscated by the police, who kept them for evidence.

When it was time for Mr. Moses to give his evidence, he told the court that he had been a friend of Morgan Blessing for at least three years. He mentioned that he had warned Blessing not to travel alone with James Barry, because of his dubious reputation, but Blessing would not listen.

Moses also identified the nugget pin as Blessing's, and mentioned that he had last seen it in the hands of a hurdy gurdy girl who swore that she had received it from James Barry.

At this time the hurdy gurdy girl was called to testify. She also identified the nugget pin, and claimed that the prisoner seemed to have lots of money to pay for dancing with the hurdies.

Following those witnesses, Dan was called to the stand, where he described finding the body of Morgan Blessing.

He was then cross examined by the lawyer, Walker, who tried to convince the jury that Dan had known the location of the body, even before Mr. Moses's went to look for it.

Dan was made to swear under oath, that he had

never before visited the site where the body was discovered. Fortunately, he was believed.

Several other witnesses maintained that while Barry could be called a gambler, he was obviously a very poor one, for he was always broke.

There were no other suspects in the case, and after numerous witnesses told of their bad experiences with James Barry, the attorney for the defense gave a speech in support of Barry.

The jury, however, were not convinced, and brought in a verdict of guilty.

"It is clear that you alone traveled with the murdered man from Quesnelmouth," said Judge Begbie to James Barry, "and that you had in your possession the weapon used to kill the man. It is also clear that after murdering him, you stripped him of all his valuable possessions, including his gold nugget pin, and his wallet containing about sixty dollars.

James Barry was sentenced to death, and was hung near the Richfield courthouse soon after. His body was interred in the Richfield cemetery.

From the courthouse Dan hurried down the hill towards town. He had to compose his notes from the trial for publication in the next days' paper. As he walked, he looked out over the valley where he could see Caenarvon Ledge, and the Welsh Company's shaft house and wheel.

'If Richard Evans did not leave Williams Creek, then he must be somewhere close at hand.' Dan said to himself. 'Could he be lost somewhere, having suffered a blow to the head perhaps, or could he have fallen down a mine shaft? For a mining man that would be most unlikely'

It was early one morning a week later when Dan returned to the office having had breakfast with Bob. He found George Wallace already at work.

"Good morning" George called. "Dan, I'm sending you on a trip to Antler Creek to do those interviews we talked about. I have arranged for a reliable horse from Mr. Mundorf, so all you have to do, is to pick up what food supplies you will need, pack some clothes, and your blankets. The trip may take several days, depending on the weather. You had better get there as soon as possible, as I received word last night that most of the miners will be leaving soon, for the winter."

On hearing this, the first thing Dan thought about was that he had to let both Collette and Bob know that he would be gone for a few days.

Later that evening as Dan made his way to the back door of the Terpsychorean Saloon, he saw Owen Parry on the street, heading in the same direction. Not wanting another confrontation, Dan turned and went into the saloon. Making his way to the dressing rooms at the back, he was stopped by James Loring, the owner.

"I thought you knew better than to come back here, you are supposed to wait outside."

"Yes I know I am not supposed to be here, but you see it is very important for me to see Collette, as I am going to be out of town for a while." stressed Dan.

"Well, just this once" said Loring, "or we will have Fanny Bendixon down on us."

Dan was fortunate to catch Collette just as she was leaving the building.

"I came this way because I know that Owen Parry is at the back door, waiting for you. I wanted you to know that I will be gone for a few days on assignment for George Wallace, to Antler Creek." said Dan as he took Collette's hand "

"Oh Dan", said Collette, almost in tears, "Owen wants to take me away with him back to Wales, and I don't want to go. What shall I do?"

"Hold Owen off, Collette, postpone any decisions until I get back, please." Dan told her. This was very distressing news for Dan, and it couldn't have come at a worse time, just as he was going to be away.

'I wonder where Owen is getting the money to be able to leave the country' Dan asked himself.

"How long will you be gone, Dan?" asked Collette.

"It will take almost a day to get to Antler, and the same to get back, but I will be as quick as I can. Perhaps four days." replied Dan.

"It will be hard to put Owen off, but I will make up some sort of excuse to wait" said Collette, taking Dan's other hand and pulling him toward her.

"Oh Dan, I don't want to marry Owen Parry, It scares me, even to be with him" she whispered as she nestled into Dan's arms.

Dan had not expected a reaction like this from Collette, and he was thrilled. He held her close for a moment, and then kissed her on the forehead.

"Come with me" he told her, "and we'll go out by the front door. You don't want to see Owen Parry at the back door, do you?" suggested Dan.

As they rushed toward the front door they passed James Loring working at his desk. He said nothing, but raised his eyebrows and shook his head.

It was early the next morning when Dan went to Mundorf's stables for the horse that he would ride on his trip to Antler Creek. It was a large horse, a brindle coloured gelding, who responded favorably to the prospect of a bit of exercise.

Loading his supplies, blankets, cooking pots and writing materials on to the horse, Dan stopped outside the Sentinel office before setting off.

"Mind you bring back some good interviews, Dan, I am counting on you, and take good care of the horse too." said George as Dan bid him farewell.

'It is nearly ten miles from Williams Creek to Antler town' said Dan to the horse, 'so we should get there about sundown, if all goes well.'

They took the trail uphill to Richfield, then continued on past McCallum Gulch and up on to the Bald Mountain. Along the way they passed dozens of men working their claims, both in the creeks and on the hillsides. The sound of shovels going through gravel, the hammering of pit props, and the echoing of loud voices filled the air.

A few miles further south the trail ran sharply uphill, to Bald Mountain, where wide open grassy slopes were occupied by small herds of sheep and cattle, their attendants watching for marauding wolves or coyotes. Off to the west Dan also noticed the trail leading to the Jack of Clubs Creek, where he had worked with Bob on his claim the year before. Here and there were clumps of short but sturdy coniferous trees, their branches growing low to the ground; nature's way of protecting the roots from the long and severe winter conditions.

Early that afternoon Bob reached Maloney's Flat, at the confluence of Grouse and Antler Creek, where he stopped to water the horse, and let it graze on the pasture-like plateau. While he ate lunch in the roadhouse, Dan was also able to have a chat with Tom Maloney, the owner.

"I have been in these parts since the first 'rush' of staking in 1861." he told Dan, "but I never did very well at mining. I decided I had a much surer way of making a living by serving the public at this site, where the pack trains stop by several times a year, on their way to Antler and Williams Creek."

Dan reached Maloney's roadhouse

Thomas Maloney, originally from Ireland, was a man in his late forties. He was a short, but sturdy individual, dark haired, and with a black beard so long he had to tuck it into his belt, to keep from tripping over it.

"I have kept my beard so that if I ever go bald" he told Dan, "I could have a wig made from it."

Maloney was very busy at the time, building a fireplace out of clay and dried grass, at one end of his roadhouse. Even as Dan saddled up his horse again, a pack train of about thirty mules arrived from Keithley Creek.

"It's Cataline", shouted Maloney from where he was working, "this will be his last trip before winter. I hope he has all the supplies I ordered."

"Where does Cataline get his supplies?" asked Dan, walking his horse up close to Maloney.

"Lillooet, usually," Maloney replied, "and sometimes as far south as San Francisco."

"Cataline", or Jean Caux, which was his real name, was originally from the Basque area between France and Spain. He had been packing supplies for the Hudson's Bay Co. since before the gold rush began. It is said that he never wrote down his orders, (possibly because he was illiterate) but kept everything in his head. He knew the cost of each item, and never forgot anything.

With a fresh start, Dan's horse trotted along with renewed vigor, across the bridge over the creek, and uphill towards Sawmill Creek.

It was one of those perfect days of fall, with a cloudless sky of azure blue, and a slight breeze that shook the golden Aspen trees. Here and there Dan noticed several small animals of the forest that were darting about, collecting nuts, and lining their nests for the coming winter. Suddenly the horse shied off the trail, and almost threw Dan off. There in the middle of the trail was a family of Franklin grouse. Strutting out in front, with his wings outstretched, and making a loud clucking sound, was the male member, a large, black feathered bird, with a big red comb that flopped about as he demonstrated his indignation at having to share the path with a horse. Behind him was his wife, a rather dull looking bird by comparison, who joined her mate in his vociferous objections, and following her were six half grown, members of the troupe.

The horse soon recovered from its scare, and stood waiting for the grouse family to depart into the underbrush.

In due time Dan and the horse arrived at Sawmill Creek, a small mining centre just south of Antler town. Here the usual sounds of a thriving community filled the air, people moving around, carts and horses driving on the trail, and the steady sound of an operating sawmill. The most distracting sound by far came from the creaking and groaning of the several water wheels turning on Antler Creek, nearly a mile way.

Strutting out in front was the male member of a family of Franklin grouse.

At Sawmill Creek about twenty buildings stood on the side hill facing a sizeable creek, and while most were built of lumber from the local mill, there was also the odd log cabin.

Pulling up at a building that had the appearance of a store, Dan tied the horse to the hitching post and walked up several steps to a short verandah. As he did so a large black dog came out of the door, barking and baring it's powerful jaws and teeth.

"Here Bingo, now you be quiet" called a male voice, and then continued.

"Hi there stranger, can we help you? As Dan turned he faced an elderly man with a shock of white hair.

Dan introduced himself, and the fact that he was a reporter, searching for the whereabouts of three gold miners.

"Well I can tell you how to find John Rose and James May, but I have not seen Ranald McDonald for a spell.

"Perhaps the other two will know where Ranald McDonald is." suggested Dan.

"Yes" said the man, "that is possible. But to find Rose and James May you continue along the trail past Sawmill Creek for another couple of miles, and then look for a log cabin on your left. That cabin belongs to them, and that's where they live, although I have heard that they are pulling out soon, for the winter."

"Well thank you so much, Sir," replied Dan, "will you give me your name, please?"

"I am Richard Baylor, I own the sawmill here, and

my wife runs the store."

"Pleased to meet you Sir, and thanks for your help" reiterated Dan.

Mounting up again, Dan continued on up the trail, and soon came across the cabin described by Baylor. Knocking on the door, he waited for some response, but when no one came, he turned and went back to the horse.

'Now what shall I do?' he asked himself. Just as he was climbing back on to the horse, he heard the sound of approaching footsteps, and someone whistling a merry tune. Waiting for a moment, it was not long before a rather tall, young man with long, brown hair appeared, and stopped when he saw Dan.

"Hello sir, are you looking for someone?" he asked in a decidedly thick Scotch brogue.

"Yes" replied Dan "I was hoping to find the miners John Rose, or James May. I believe this is their cabin."

"Yes, it is" and I am John Rose, who are you?" he asked.

Dan introduced himself and explained why he was there.

"Come into the cabin, Dan, and we will have a chat while I make some coffee."

The interior of the log cabin was a typical batchelor's abode, with piles of this and that all over the place. Only the small combination heater and cook-stove, in the middle of the dirt floor, and two bunks on the east wall, remained visable and uncovered. On the west wall was a small window covered over with the thin skin from an animal's stomach.

As John brewed coffee, he and Dan discussed the events that had led him to find gold on Antler Creek.

"Well", said John, "Ranald McDonald, James May and I, had mined together at Lillooet in '58, where we did rather well, but we knew there had to be something even better north of there.

An American, Arron Post, had gone prospecting up the Fraser River in 1858, as far as the mouth of the Chilcotin River. When he returned to Victoria and was interviewed by the Times Colonist newspaper, he gave a report of his trip, and said that the further he went upriver, the larger the gold."

Why didn't he go any further?" asked Dan.

"He ran out of supplies" replied John.

"Where are your other two partners?" asked Dan, "I am hoping to interview them also."

"Ranald has sold his claims, and left for the south a week ago, but Jim May is still here. We are both going south in a few days."

As they sat drinking their black coffee, Dan noticed John's shirt, which was made of deerskin.

"Did you bring that with you from California?" asked Dan, as he fingered the soft brown hide.

"No, as a matter of fact my mother made it for me, before I left Scotland, there are lots of deer there."

"So you came to the Cariboo from Scotland?" asked Dan.

"Wrong again", said John with a chuckle, "I was

166

only a child when I left Scotland for California in 1842. My mother has a well to do brother there, and I was sent to live with them, and go to school there. When gold was discovered in California in 1848, just as I left school, I did well at mining there, but I have not yet been back to Scotland to see my mother; perhaps now I will.

"I guess Antler Creek was very rich when you first discovered it?" Dan asked, expecting John to balk at this question, but that did not happen.

"At first we recovered 200 ounces a day, each, with our rockers." disclosed John. "Now, we are each making about $100. a day."

"Enough to keep you for the rest of your life", remarked Dan.

"Oh it was not the money that we came for," disclosed John, "but for the sheer excitement of the discovery."

"Well thank you very much for allowing me to interview you," said Dan as he rose to leave, "where do you suppose I could find Jim May?"

"Well, if you are not in too much of a hurry, just wait here for a while, he is bound to come along before dark."

As time passed, and Jim May did not appear, John began to prepare a supper of some trout that he had caught that afternoon, and some wild greens. At the same time Dan began to think about his horse that had been patiently waiting outside.

"Do you have a barn somewhere near here John?"

asked Dan

"Oh yes, that's right, you came on horseback, didn't you. Yes, we have a sort of a barn. Well, it's what we call a 'wicky up', a shelter made of branches and clay from the creek, but it does provide some protection from the weather. You will find it down by the creek, out of the wind."

Taking his horse by the bridle, Dan led it down to the creek to drink, and then put it into the small shelter, where he dispensed some hay that he had brought in a sack.

"This will have to do you tonight, horse, it looks like we'll be staying over."

Back at the cabin John Rose was getting concerned.

"It's not like Jim to be out after dark" he mentioned to Dan, "I wonder if he went visiting somewhere. Usually he lets me know if he is going to be away. If he is still not back after supper, I will go to look for him."

Just then there was a rattle at the door, and in walked a tired, middle aged man with a pack on his back, and a gold pan under his arm. It was Jim May.

"I was getting worried about you." John Rose told him.

"You will never guess where I have been, John" he said, taking off his pack and putting down his gold pan.

"Where?" asked John.

"I was with Bill Cunningham all day, and we discovered good gold showings on a creek to the south east of here. I am not going to stake it, it is Bill's discovery really, but it was interesting to find another new discovery."

"Did you bring back some samples?" asked John.

"Yes, yes," replied Jim, reaching for his pack.

Out of the sack came a handful of quartz rock with wide bands of gold across them. The gold was a greenish colour, indicating a percentage of copper.

"Jim," said John, "we have a guest here this evening, this is young Dan McDermott, a reporter from the Cariboo Sentinel on Williams Creek. He would like to interview you."

"Now what would you want to interview me for?" Jim May asked.

Dan, who was getting very hungry, was hoping that supper would not be delayed for too long, replied.

"You and your associates are famous now, for discovering the rich gold on Antler Creek, and my boss, George Wallace, who owns the newspaper, has sent me up here to interview you."

"I think we will eat supper first" announced John Rose, "before it gets cold."

After supper, and while Jim was washing the dishes, Dan helped to dry them.

"I understand you are an American, Jim" ventured Dan, "and that you were born in the southern States."

"Yes" said Jim, "on a farm in Tennessee. My father decided to move to Iowa when I was fifteen, because he felt that Tennessee was getting too crowded.

"Obviously your father liked the wide open spaces"

suggested Dan.

"Oh yes," agreed Jim. "By 1848 we had settled on another farm near Troy, in Iowa, where I helped to clear the land, and planted corn. The next spring we heard about gold in California, and I left home to get some.

Travelling across the wilderness between Iowa and California was very dangerous at that time.

On more than one occasion we had to defend ourselves from marauding Indians when our caravan was attacked. One of my closest friends was killed and scalped.

"That must have been a terrifying experience" said Dan.

"When we finally reached California it was hard to find a claim, the country was so overcrowded with prospectors. Later we managed to get mining on a worthwhile claim, and made lots of money. Following that I traveled back home, and gave my family a fair share of my earnings, well, at least they would never again want for anything.

Then my buddies and I heard about gold on the Fraser River, in Canada, British Columbia. We traveled by way of the Columbia River, and reached the Thompson River in the spring of 1859. At Nicomen, a tributary of the Thompson, prospectors were arriving every day, and the gold there was rich for a short time.

"I have heard that the Indians in Washington Territory were killing off the American prospectors along the border." mentioned Dan.

"Yes, we had some very scary moments going

through there" continued Jim May. "From there we went to Lillooet, where I met John Rose, Ranald McDonald, and an Englishman named Billy Barker, who were all mining there".

"That fall John and I decided we would not wait for spring, but go north as soon as possible. We had heard other prospectors planning to go upriver, and wanting to be the first to discover the best gold, we left Lillooet, and traveled upriver, John, Ranald, George Weaver, 'Doc' Keithley, John McLean, Bill Cunningham, and myself."

"It was tough going, and hard to find enough to eat. We got tired of fish, and although grouse were easy to trap, we hated to kill them, as they have their chicks in the spring. Later, John Rose shot a Caribou, and then we ate well. Prospecting our way along, we found quite a bit of gold on the Quesnelle River, and also up on the banks beside the river. We had just reached the forks of the river, when winter overtook us.

The timber was very thick on the flat there, and we managed to build ourselves a cabin, where we survived until spring.

That spring hundreds of miners came upriver, and settled at the Forks of the Quesnelle River. Our party soon left there to go prospecting.

'Doc' Keithley was the first to strike it rich on a creek to the north east of Quesnelle Forks, a big creek that flows into a large lake. In the meantime the rest of us continued to prospect, and climbed up a creek four miles from the lake, to where George Weaver made a rich discovery. We kept climbing and prospecting, over French Snowshoe and Little Snowshoe Mountain until we discovered Antler Creek."

"It was late fall when we came across the sun burned nuggets sticking out of the dirt on the side of the creek. We couldn't believe it at first, the gold was so plentiful"

"Gosh that must have been exciting" said Dan, sitting on the edge of his seat.

"There were also a lot of antlers of 'Caribou' on the ground near the creek, and for want of a better name, we called our rich find 'Antler Creek', the rest you already know."

Dan was fascinated with Jim May's account, and spent some time working on his notes, so as not to leave anything out of the exciting story.

"Would you like to come down to the creek tomorrow, to watch us mining?" asked John.

"I would love to" replied Dan, "but I should be getting back to Williams Creek. George Wallace will be looking for me. By the way, did you know that we have a mystery going on in Williams Creek? I don't suppose you have seen anything of a man by the name of Richard Evans?" Dan related some of the circumstances, but John Rose and Jim May shook their heads.

After an early breakfast Dan said goodbye to the two miners, and thanked them for their hospitality.

"We will be on the look out for the missing man." said John as he and Jim shook hands with Dan.

CHAPTER 10

The Moving Corpse

Returning by the same route, Dan reached Williams Creek early that evening, where he first returned the horse back to Mundorf's stables, and told the owner, Joseph, that he had never ridden on such a pleasant tempered animal before.

At the office of the Sentinel Dan found George Wallace working away, preparing all the advertisements for the next paper.

"It's a good thing you went to Antler Creek when you did, it would probably be too late next week." remarked George.

"True" said Dan. "By the way, have there been any new developments in the missing mine manager case?"

"Not that I have heard" replied George.

"Is there any rush for these interviews tonight?" asked Dan.

"No" replied George," tomorrow will do."

"Right now I am going to have some dinner, and find Bob over at the 'Jake'"said Dan "he may know the latest news, if there is any."

"I will finish writing up these two interviews tomorrow morning" he told George, "and then I am going to have a talk with Henry Fitzgerald, the police-

173

man" Dan told George.

'That young man would make a good detective' said George to himself, 'he is persistent, and seems determined to get to the bottom of the mystery'

At the 'Wake Up Jake' restaurant Dan expected to find Bob, but instead he found Collette, who was about to leave for work.

"Dan, you're back! How was your trip?" she exclaimed as she came over to Dan's table, and gave him a hug.

They talked for a few minutes. "I have not seen Owen for several days, Dan." said Collette, "I am hoping he will postpone any immediate plans of marriage." she went on, "I suppose he must be very busy."

Just then Bob turned up, and welcomed Dan back from his trip.

"There is something very strange going on" he told Dan and Collette, "No one has seen Owen Parry for the last three days, apparently not even Beavan Jones."

Collette let out a gasp and looked horrified at the news, although Dan noticed that emotionally, she was not as disturbed as he would have expected.

"Has anyone checked his cottage?" asked Dan, "or informed the police, for instance?"

"Yes" said Bob, the police have been notified."

"Well," said Dan, "this is getting serious. Now we have two missing men. "I must have a chat with Beavan, to see what he has to say."

When Dan told George Wallace the news, he was very concerned, and asked Dan to write an article about it for the paper.

"Also, don't forget we have the stage coach arriving tomorrow, with Governor Seymour aboard, Dan" said George, "he is coming to visit the miners here on Williams and Lightning Creek. I want you to go along with the entourage to report on the visit."

Dan had forgotten about the Govenor's visit, and wished that he could stay at home to investigate the mystery of the now two missing men. He also wanted to spend some time interviewing Ned Stout, the miner on Lowhee Mountain, and Neamiah Smith, another miner.

'But then I must not forget how lucky I am to have this job' he reminded himself.

The next afternoon as Dan left the office of the Sentinel he could hear the sounds of Barnard's stagecoach arriving down the street. Pulling out his pocket watch he looked at it and thought 'and just on time, too.'

Down from the coach stepped several gentleman dressed in dark suits, and bowler hats on their heads. On hand to meet this distinguished group was Gold Commissioner Peter O'Reilly, who had arrived by special carriage from Quesnelle Mouth the evening before.

Dan walked briskly down the street, and caught up with the visitors just as they climbed the steps up to the Hotel de France. By listening to the conversations, he came to realize that following a gala dinner at the hotel, the guests would be attending a performance of the Amateur Dramatic Society that evening, to be held in

Fanny Bendixon's 'Parlour Saloon'.

That evening Dan donned a waistcoat and dark jacket, borrowed from George Wallace, and sat in the back row of the theatre, where he observed the performance entitled "The Golden Bracelet" a melodrama from the previous century. The actors and performers were men of the town and their wives Mr. James Godwin and his wife Jean, Mr. Edwin Jones and his wife Margaret, and two batchelors, James Anderson, and a William Barry, who had a strong tenor voice.

The next morning, after a sumptuous breakfast, the entourage, with Dan following behind, traveled south through the Chinese section of the community.

In honor of the Governor's visit, the Chinese population had decorated their stores, restaurants, and even the street, with evergreen boughs, and erected placards in Chinese characters, welcoming the governor to Williams Creek. Governor Seymour was so impressed that he insisted on pausing to speak with one or two Chinese representatives.

"How is business here?" he asked of a tall, slim Chinese man wearing a long, padded coat.

"Velly good, Sir, we deal mostly with our own people, except for the laundries."

"Don't any of you work as cooks in the white restaurants?"

"Yes, that is true, but only men."

"Do you have any Chinese women here?" the governor asked.

"No, it is too expensive for us to have any of our

women in Canada, Sir. We would have to pay a large head tax."

"Then it must be very lonely for you" said the governor. I will bring this point up in parliament."

Before leaving Chinatown, a young Chinese boy, Martin Chung, the same one that had picked up Dan's laundry, presented Governor Seymour with a gift from the community. The governor opened the newspaper wrapped parcel, and held up a green porcelain cup and saucer, decorated with red dragons.

Thank you so much" he said, "I shall treasure it always."

As the entourage proceeded up Bald Mountain, Dan had to stop his horse every now and again to allow him to write his notes.

"Just where are we going?" Dan asked one of the governor's aides.

"To visit the miners on Lightning Creek, I understand" he replied. "I hear the gold there is even richer than on Williams Creek"

"Is that a fact" said Dan, "How long is the governor expected to remain in the Cariboo?" Dan asked further.

"Just for today" the man told him, "he will not return to Williams Creek, but will continue south from Van Winkle."

On the way up Bald Mountain to the headwaters of Williams Creek, the governor stopped and visited several mines. The Diller, the Steadman, the San Juan, and the Deadwood, where their owners offered the governor nuggets as gifts, but where he would not accept any, for fear of being accused of taking a bribe.

Having reached Summit Rock, an outcropping of bedrock at the 5000ft above sea level, the trail turned south west over Mount Agnes and proceeded towards Lightning Creek.

By this time everyone was getting hungry, having been out in the fresh air all morning, and in such a high altitude.

At Dunbar Flats they arrived at Beedy and Lindhard's roadhouse, where they stopped and enjoyed a meal of beefsteak pie, rice pudding, and tea. Daniel was thankful to have been included as part of the entourage, and did not have to pay for his meal.

Josiah Beedy and Joachim Lindhard, the owners, were there for the governor's visit. and seemed willing to give Dan small interviews.

During the early 1860s these two noteworthy entrepreneurs, Josiah C. Beedy and Joachim "Henry" Lindhard had been very active on Lightning Creek.

Both had been pioneers of 1858 when they mined, owned stores, and packed supplies to all the main gold centres, from Port Douglas to Williams Creek.

On Lighting Creek they had both made considerable contributions to the advancement of modern mining methods.

Lindhard and his associates in the Van Winkle Company implemented a plan for a bedrock drain, which made it possible for all claim holders on the creek to pump the water out of their deep shafts.

Josiah Beedy, who was also a member of the Van Winkle Company, had his own 'hill claims' on Burns Mountain, where he installed one of the first stamp mills in the country.

As partners they operated roadhouses at Van Winkle, Dunbar Flats, and Fontaine Creek.

After dinner the governor and his entourage drove to the community of Van Winkle, where he visited several other mines, and gave an address to the miners. He congratulated them for their great success at mining, and extolled the fact that their successful efforts added greatly to the economy of the province. Dan, who heard the speech, listened closely, and copied it word for word, into his notebook.

Following the governor's address and his immediate departure for Quesnelemouth, Dan turned his horse around and headed back up the trail to Williams Creek.

Not far from Dunbar Flats he came to Eagle Creek, near the headwaters of Lightning Creek.

Just as he rounded the corner of the trail, he noticed that his horse had gone lame. Dismounting, he examined the horse's hooves, and realized that the shoe on the front right foot had come off.

Having seen a second trail veering off from the upper side of the main trail, Dan led his horse for a few yards, and then around a corner where the land opened up onto a flat. There he could see a house, and close by it, a mine shaft.

Knocking on the door, it was opened by a very tall

and handsome, middle aged Englishman.

"Good evening young man" he said as he greeted Dan.

"I am sorry to bother you" said Dan "but my horse has lost a shoe, and I have a long ride ahead of me, back to Williams Creek. Do you happen to have some blacksmithing equipment, and a spare shoe?"

"My dear Sir" replied the man, bowing low in front of Dan, "William Houseman has everything, including a horse's shoe" and he started to quote, in flowery fashion,.

"For want of a nail the shoe was lost,
For want of a shoe the horse was lost
For want of a horse the rider was lost
For want of a rider the battle was lost
For want of a battle the kingdom was lost
And all for the want of a horseshoe nail!

"That is a very old quotation" he said, "and who might you be?"

Dan explained what he was doing there, and then went with William Houseman to his barn, which also served as a blacksmith shop. In one corner of the building they picked out the right shoe, and in another corner they found the tools to nail it on.

"Now that that's done" said Houseman, would you care to have tea with me?"

"I would love to" said Dan, but it's getting late, and I had better be on my way. I really appreciate your help, though, I would have been in a sad state otherwise."

"Oh that was alright" he said, looking rather disappointed at Dan's reluctance to remain "Yes, I admit, I wouldn't be surprised to see winter arrive any day now. I hope you will be alright going over the mountain."

"Goodbye Sir" called Dan as he started off.

As the trail rose up the mountain, a cold wind got up, and before long developed into a driving gale, accompanied by a flurry of sleet. Dan was wearing a warm coat, but being without a hat, the wind blew the sleet down his collar, and over his head and face. The horse too, in trying to avoid the wind, wrapped its tail around itself.

'I wonder how long this is going to last' Dan asked himself. Turning the horse around, he could see the source of the storm coming over the mountain from the west. Realizing that it was getting worse, he looked around for any possible shelter, a tree, or a building.

As the storm became progressively worse, and with the sleet coming down in sheets, it became hard to see anything more than a few feet away.

In the distance, close to the timber, Dan thought he could see what looked like a building. Guiding his horse across the open mountainside, he drew close to where he thought he had seen a building.

It was a log cabin, a very old cabin, for the clay chinking between the logs had long since fallen out, and the chimney, made of hydraulic pipe, lay abandoned, across the shake roof.

'The horse and I will get in there' thought Dan. 'At least we will be under cover and out of the storm', he decided. Dismounting, he tried to open the door. It was stiff, and the hinges creaked when it opened. When he tried to lead the horse inside, it balked, and refused to enter.

"Come on boy, get in there, it will be dry." persuaded Dan.

It was a few minutes before he managed to get the horse into the cabin, and just as he tied the animal up to a post, Dan saw a glint of something shining in the dirt on the floor. Fingering around in the dusty soil, he found it, and picked it up. He was astonished to find that it was an old gold coin, a $10 gold piece, that looked just like the one he had lost some time ago; the one he had been given as a christening present when he was a baby.

Turning the coin over, he read the inscription, "For Daniel, from his grandfather, February 2, 1847."

'Owen Parry', he said to himself, 'I always did suspect that he had stolen it when we were coming down the river on the barge.'

But that was not all that Dan found in the cabin.

One of the first things he had noticed upon entering, was the large metal heater in the middle of the room, and the fact that the door of the heater seemed to be bulging.

As Dan brushed past it, the door suddenly flew open, and out rolled the decomposing body of a man! It was Richard Evans, the missing mine owner!

'Oh my God' said Dan, as he froze in disbelief, 'so this is where he ended up. Someone has murdered the poor man! Was it Owen Parry?'

Out rolled the decomposing body of Richard Evans.

'I wondered what the strange smell was in here', thought Dan, 'no wonder the horse balked. Of course it would be a lot worse, if the temperature was not close to freezing.' Without touching it, Dan looked closely at the corpse, and could see that Richard Evans had been stabbed several times in the back, and in the chest.

It was very hard for Dan to remain in the same room with the corpse, but he did not have any choice, for outside the storm was still raging. Fortunately, there was a window in the cabin, which Dan managed to open, that allowed a cold, fresh wind to blow through.

The old cabin had not been lived in for a long time, for cobwebs and thick layers of dust had taken possession of everything. At one end were the remains of a metal cook stove, although most of the lids were gone, and out of the firebox, a heap of ashes had spilled out on to the ground. Beside the stove was a broken down sideboard, with a few metal dishes on the shelves. In another corner was a wooden bed frame, without any mattress or springs, and on the dirt floor, a heap of discarded clothing.

'I am not going to touch anything' said Dan to himself, ' I will go straight to the policeman when I get home, if I get home.' he thought.

About an hour later, after darkness had fallen, the storm subsided, leaving an inch of wet snow on the ground.

'I am going to try to find my way back home' said Dan to himself, 'I'm not staying here all night with a corpse. I am sure the horse will know his way home.'

The horse seemed only too pleased to leave the cabin, and as Dan climbed up on it, it started off, over the mountain, towards Williams Creek.

It was close to midnight when Dan reached the town. The street was still, with not even one light showing in the buildings. He wondered what to do with the horse, but when he took it to Mundorf's stables, he found it still open.

Leading the horse in, he put it into an empty stall, tied it up to the crib, and gave it some hay, before he left.

Down the street at the Sentinel office the door was locked. 'Now what shall I do?' Dan wondered.

The only solution he could think of was to go back to the stables, and spend the rest of the night there. Nestled into some hay up in the loft, Dan was warm, but found it hard to settle down; the events of the last day had been so horrifying.

'Did Owen Parry kill Richard Evans? he asked himself. 'How else would his gold piece have got into the cabin?' Finally he fell asleep, but it was a troubled sleep, full of dreams that made no sense.

As morning came the sound of voices and animals moving around in the stables below, woke Dan up. It was broad daylight, and he was hungry.

Making his way down the ladder Dan went first to the Sentinel office, but it was obviously still too early for George Wallace to be there. Dan pulled out his pocket watch, it said six thirty. Noticing that there were lights on in the "Wake Up Jake" restaurant, he went in to get some breakfast.

"You are the first customer this morning", mentioned the waiter,

"What are you doing up so early?" he asked, but of course Dan was not about to tell him his gruesome story.

With a hot cup of coffee, and some oatmeal porridge in his stomach, the world began to look better to Dan.

CHAPTER 11

A Second Man Missing

Walking over to the Police office, Dan found
Corporal McPherson nursing a cup of coffee and
chewing on a bun,

"Sergeant Fitzgerald will be here soon, can I help
you?" he asked.

"I would like to report that I have found the body of
the missing mine manager, Richard Evans. He has been
dead for some time, stabbed in the back and chest."

The Corporal's eyes grew large and his mouth flew
open, "What?" he said at last, almost choking on his
bun. When Dan told him how he had happened to discover the body, his eyes grew even larger.

"I also found this old $10. gold coin at the site, and
believe it or not, I am sure it is mine." As soon as Dan
said this, he wished he hadn't, for now he too, was im-
plicated.

"Where is this coin?" asked the policeman?"

"Here", said Dan as he placed it on the desk.

"What makes you think it is yours?" the policeman
asked again. Dan showed him the inscription, and explained how he had been given the coin. There was also
the fact that it had disappeared from his pack, months
before.

Just then the Sergeant arrived. When he heard

187

Dan's story, he praised him for reporting his findings so promptly, and for not touching anything at the scene of the discovery. When he heard about the gold coin, he gave Dan a strange look.

"We will keep the coin for now" he told Dan, "and I don't want to hear that you have left Williams Creek until we have made sure of the identity of the murderer."

When Dan returned to the Sentinel office he found George Wallace up to his elbows in printer's ink, running off the latest copy of the paper. Beside him was the young Chinese boy, Martin Chung, who had arrived to deliver some laundry, but who had remained to help George.

"Dan, you're back at last, I was going to send out a search party for you. What delayed you? You should have been back before dark last night."

Dan explained what had happened, the horse losing it's shoe, the storm, the cabin, and last but not least, his discovery of the body of Richard Evans.

George Wallace looked aghast at Dan's story, and almost accused him of making it up.

"No, no, its all true, I have already been to the police.

"Who is going to tell Mrs. Evans?" asked George.

Before anyone could answer that question, Sergeant Fitzgerald arrived at the door.

"Daniel McDermott, I want you to take me to the cabin where you discovered the body of Richard Evans" he announced.

188

"Right now?" asked Dan.

"Yes, immediately" replied the policeman, "we must locate the body. and bring it back to Mrs. Evans for identification."

Mounted on horses, with a spare one following behind, Dan and Sergeant Fitzgerald left Williams Creek and rode up onto the Bald Mountain. It had snowed several inches overnight, making the trail virtually invisible, except for recognizable landmarks of stunted trees and rocks.

As they started down the trail to Lightning Creek, Dan tried to remember just where he had seen the log cabin. It had been a miracle that he had seen it at all, the sleet storm was so heavy that evening.

As they wandered to and fro, searching, the Sergeant was getting impatient, and Dan knew he was beginning to think that he had made up the story.

Suddenly, as the sun came out from behind a cloud, Dan saw it, the little, old log cabin, all by itself, beside the stunted timber.

"There it is!" called Dan, as he urged his horse on. As they reached the building, they tied their horses to the trees at the back. It took some pulling and adjustment of the door to get it open before they could enter. As Dan stood inside the doorway, he sensed that something had changed since he had been there. The dirt floor had been smoothed over with tree branches, obliterating any footprints that had once been there. As he looked further, Dan suddenly realized that the body that had rolled out of the heater, the murdered body of

Richard Evans, was no longer there! Walking over to the heater, Dan opened the door, and looked in, but it was empty, save for a few ashes in the bottom.

"So, where is the body you saw yesterday?" asked the Sergeant.

"I can't believe that it is gone" Dan exclaimed. "I tell you, when I left the cabin yesterday, the body was there, in front of the heater, where it had rolled out."

"Where did you find the gold coin?" asked the policeman.

"In the dirt, close to the door of the heater" explained Dan, "whoever put the body in the heater, must have had to work hard to get it in, and the coin fell out of their pocket." suggested Dan.

"Well", said the Sergeant, "either you dreamed this whole story up, or someone was here after you left. They have certainly removed all the evidence."

After several more minutes spent looking around the cabin, the policeman decided that they should leave.

"We are not doing much good here" he told Dan.

As Dan held the cabin door open for the policeman, he happened to look along the rough edges on the side, and there, hanging from a splinter of wood, was a scrap of woolen cloth. Examining it closely, Dan recognized it as having come off the heather coloured tweed jacket worn by Richard Evans!

Without disturbing it, he called to Sergeant Fitzgerald, "Come back and look at this, Sir!"

"See here", said Dan as he pointed out the scrap

of torn cloth. "It has come from the dead man's jacket, probably caught there as the murderer was removing the body."

"Well, well, you are very observant, I must say", exclaimed the Sergeant as he carefully removed the evidence from the door, and put it into his wallet.

"Good for you, Dan," he said further, "You would make a very good detective. If you ever get tired of your job at the 'Sentinel', let me know."

I shall visit Mrs. Evans immediately, to verify that the cloth came from her husband's jacket."

Dan began to feel a lot better after that. 'At least the Sergeant is beginning to believe me' he thought.

As Dan and the policeman neared Williams Creek, the Sergeant said,

"Please do not mention this trip, or anything to do with this investigation to anyone, until we have completed our findings, and most definitely do not publish anything in the paper."

"So how did that go?" asked George Wallace as Dan entered the 'Sentinel' office.

"I am sworn not to divulge any information about it, at least not for the present" Dan told him.

"Well, now that you are here, perhaps we can get back to working on the paper." said George with a little note of sarcasm," I still want you to get those two interviews done before Ned Stout and 'Blackjack' Smith leave for the winter."

"Yes Sir," Dan agreed, I shall arrange to meet with

them as soon as possible."

That afternoon Dan walked up to Richfield to see Collette, and on the way back he would attempt to see Ned Stout at his mine.

Collette was in the kitchen of her home making a cake when Dan walked in..

They discussed the disappearance of Owen Parry.

"I am beginning to think this has something to do with the mine, the Welsh Company mine" said Collette, "I would think that Beavan Jones is trembling in his boots, for fear he might be the next to disappear."

"Have you ever suspected Beavan as the murderer?" asked Dan.

Oh no" said Collette "why would you suspect him?"

"The last time I spoke to Beavan, some time ago now, he told me that things were not going too well at the mine, and that they may be closing down soon. He also told me that some gold was missing."

"Oh my", exclaimed Collette, "Let's you and I go up to the mine, Dan, and have a talk with Beavan. I would not think of going alone to speak with him, except that as Owen Parry's fiance, I feel some responsibility." suggested Collette.

"Yes, I will go with you, but not for a few days;" said Dan, "I have been away from my work so much lately, that I am getting behind. Perhaps next week?"

"Yes, that would be fine." Collette replied.

As Dan sat watching Collette finish making a cake, Collette's mother, Mrs. Dumais came into the room.

192

Seeing Dan, she gave a little 'huff', and took a seat by the window.

"Do you have any notion of where Owen Parry could be?" she asked Dan, "Collette and I are both very upset over his disappearance. As you know, he and Collette were to be married soon, and I have even begun to sew a dress for Collette's wedding."

"Now, now, mother", interrupted Collette, "don't get yourself upset again. The police are investigating, and there is really nothing we can do, except wait".

"I am getting tired of waiting" replied Mrs. Dumais," her voice rising several tones higher.

"With Collette married to a rich miner I was looking forward to returning to Paris" she exclaimed, her voice now reaching almost a hysterical pitch.

Collette attempted to calm her mother by offering her a cup of coffee, which took her mind off the offending subject.

"Are you still dancing at the saloon?" Dan asked Collette.

"No, the German girls left for California last week, so I am out of a job. Things are very quiet around town now, even the miners are preparing to leave for the winter."

Leaving Collette and her mother arguing over the mystery of Owen Parry's disappearance, Dan went over to Ned Stout's mine, where he was told that Stout was in Quesnelle Mouth, but would be back in a day or two.

That evening Dan called in at the 'Wake Up Jake'

restaurant, hoping to see Bob Chase. With all the trouble at the Welsh Co. mine, Dan wondered if Bob was still working.

As Dan sat waiting, he saw Beavan Jones come in off the street. Beavan sat down at a table by himself, so Dan walked across and asked if he could join him.

"By all means, young man. What's this rumour I have heard, that you have found the body of Richard Evans ?"

'Goodness,' thought Dan, 'how did that news get out?'

"I am sorry Beavan, but I have been warned by the police not to talk about that subject."

"Oh" exclaimed Beavan, with suprisingly little emotion, "I have been talking to Mrs. Evans, and she tells me that she and Richard were soon to have a divorce. Apparently Richard was having an affair with a woman here on the creek."

"I'm sorry" repeated Dan, "I know nothing of Mr. and Mrs. Evans's personal life."

On seeing Bob Chase arrive, Dan excused himself, and went to meet Bob. They hugged each other as they met.

"Good to see you, old pal" said Dan. "I have been so busy lately, I haven't had time to keep up with what you have been doing. Are you still working?"

"Yes, I am working," Bob told him, "but not with the Welsh Co. of course. I bought some shares in the Cameron claim, and that's where I've been working."

The two friends visited for quite a while over several cups of coffee, and Dan found it extremely hard to keep from telling Bob of his discovery of Richard Evans. Bob sensed that Dan was holding something back from him, and finally Dan had to tell him that he had promised not to speak of it.

"I am going to be very busy for a few days" he told Bob, "I have to interview two pioneer miners, before they leave for the winter."

"That's a good idea, said Bob, "You never know what might happen to them over the winter."

It was the next day when Dan climbed up Lowhee Mountain to see Ned Stout. While it was still the same mountain, the Welsh Company claims were on the east side, while Stout's mine was on the west, along a deep gulch, and a little to the south.

As Dan drew close to the mine, he could see Ned Stout standing beside the water wheel, a small man with a handle bar moustache half hidden by a Cossack type fur hat. Dressed in denim overalls, worn over a thick padded jacket, on his feet were felt boots with fur tops.

It would appear that the several men working with Stout were preparing the mine for a winter shutdown. The very large wooden water wheel near the shaft house was being jacked up, to prevent it from freezing in its normal operating position, several feet under ground.

"Good morning Sir," said Dan as he greeted Ned Stout. "I have been sent by the Editor of the Sentinel newspaper to interview you. I can see that you are busy, and perhaps I should come at a more convenient time."

"Oh no young sir, actually I was just going to stop for lunch. Perhaps you would care to join me in the shaft house?" he asked.

"That would be ideal, sir." said Dan.

The shaft house had been built of lumber sawn from a mill at Antler Creek, and was insulated with old newspapers.

"I suppose they are old 'Sentinel' newspapers." commented Dan"

"What better use for old newspapers?" asked Mr. Stout.

It was warm in the shaft house, where a fire in an iron cookstove was crackling away, and where a kettle full of water was steaming over a back lid.

"Do you drink coffee?" asked Stout.

"Yes, a good hot drink for a cold day" replied Dan.

Out of the oven Ned Stout removed several hot meat pies, and offered one to Dan.

"I buy these from Mrs. Evans, she calls them 'Cornish Pasties', made from the meat of local Caribou." commented Stout.

"I wonder who shot the Caribou", asked Dan.

"I did" said Stout, "How do you like it? I shot one just last week, up over Mount Agnes, there's a small herd of them over there."

"That's very interesting" said Dan, "I thought they had become extinct."

Ned Stout spoke with a heavy German accent, but his words were very well enunciated.

"I gather you were born in Germany, sir?" asked Dan, as he got out his pencil and note book.

"I was born in 1827, and traveled to New York, America, when I was just nineteen. A few years later I heard about the California gold rush, and joined a wagon train going across country.

We had to fight Indian war parties along the way, but I managed to survive. The gold in California was rich, and we all made lots of money.

By 1858 I had the gold fever bad, and went on to the Fraser River rush in British Columbia. The gold on the river was very fine, and hard to catch, but we were looking for big nuggets, which we were told could be found upriver at Lillooet.

As we traveled up the canyons, we were attacked by hostile tribes of Indians, hundreds of them, who killed several of our miners every day.

They attacked us with poison arrows, and I have many of the scars all over my body, where I was attacked.

Fortunately we had a clever doctor with us, and he saved many of us from dying, including me.

Finally we grew tired of being attacked, so we banded together, and waged a three day war against the Indians, until we reached an agreement with the chiefs, and were allowed to return to our mining claims.

By 1859 a lot of us were traveling up the Fraser River as far as the Quesnel River, and to Quesnel

Forks. From there we got to Keithley Creek, and then to Williams Creek. My partner was 'Dutch Bill' Dietz, after whom Williams Creek is named.

I discovered rich gold here by following Richard Willoughby past his claims on the other side of Lowhee Mountain. I was also the one who persuaded Billy Barker to dig below the canyon on Williams Creek. You see I had done some prospecting, and found that there are no less than three different stratas of gold in this valley."

"How long do you predict the gold will last on your claim, sir?"

"At least another five years, I hope." said Stout as he made some more coffee. "So far I have dug and recovered the weight of myself and my dog, in gold. That's about two hundred and fifty pounds."

Dan was very impressed with what Stout had told him, and it made him a little envious.

"Thank you very much, sir, I will not keep you from your work any longer, and thank you so much for lunch." said Dan as he left.

Back down the mountain, Dan hurried on to the newspaper office to write up his interview. George Wallace seemed very pleased with what he read

"Ned Stout must have a strong constitution to have survived all his adversities." mentioned George.

"I have noticed that German people are strong minded, and do not give up easily." said Dan.

"When are you planning on going to see Nehemiah Smith, Dan? George asked, "I hear he is leaving for the south in a few days."

"I could go today, if you don't need me here" replied Dan.

"Yes, I think you should, before winter sets in." replied George.

As Dan trudged up the road he passed through Chinatown, where he saw Martin, the Chinese boy whose father owned one of the several laundries.

"How are you doing Martin, have you been working at the newspaper office lately?" asked Dan.

"Yes, Mr. Dan, two times last week" he replied. "Mr. George, he very good to me."

"The newspaper business is a good one to learn, Martin, you watch how everything is done, and learn."

"First I need to learn to read and write English" said the lad, "you think you could teach me?"

"I could lend you some books, and work with you when I have time." suggested Dan.

"Very good, Mr. Dan," said Martin, "I wait to see you again." he called as Dan continued on his walk.

The mining activity up Williams Creek and beyond had subsided noticeably, even since the week before, when Dan had gone to Lightning Creek with the Governor's entourage.

Almost all of the hundreds of claims along the way lay silent, the miners had gone, their tools and equipment put under cover for the winter.

As he neared the canyon, Dan could hear the sound of activity, and several voices, not too far away.

'Ah ha', thought Dan, 'someone's still here.'

"You two, pack that set of tools into the storage cabin," said one voice, and "pile those boots into the other cabin" said another male voice.

Walking downhill to the open pit of the mine, Dan could see several men working, and one of them was Nehemiah Smith, the owner of the Black Jack Hill mine. Dan knew this, because he had once heard him speak at the miner's meetings at the Cambrian Hall.

"Hello there young man" called Smith when he saw Dan, "what are you doing here?"

Dan explained the reason for his visit, and requested an interview.

"I'm terribly busy right now, as you can see; going to leave on Friday's coach for California. Be back next spring, though, can you wait 'til then?

"My boss will box my ears if I don't get an interview from you today" complained Dan, "It won't take long, just give me the bare essentials, and I can fill in the details."

That's what I am afraid of," said Smith in a sarcastic tone, "you newspaper men always exaggerate. Well alright, but only for a few minutes, we have to get this stuff put away before nightfall.

As Dan took out his notebook, he and Smith sat down on a pile of lumber, close to Smith's claim.

"Well" said Smith as he wiped his brow with a rag from his pocket. "I was born in a small town in Maryland, in the U.S. of A., but my parents took me with them to Ohio when I was just a youngster.

My mother died when I was twelve, and my father

was married again, to a woman I could not abide. So I ran away to sea when I was about fourteen. I stayed at sea until 1858, when I heard of the gold rush in British Columbia. At Lillooet I met my good friend Thomas Latham, commonly known as 'Dancing Bill'. Bill and I were partners on a claim and made about $3500 together, over the winter.

The next year, 1860, Bill and I went to Keithley Creek, in the Cariboo, where we made over $10,000 in just a year. Shortly after that Bill and I, and three other miners worked on Nelson Creek, a tributary of Slough Creek, where we made over $16,000 in about six weeks.

"Why was Thomas Latham called 'Dancing Bill?' asked Dan.

"He loved to dance, and was really good at it, especially tap dancing, in fact he would dance at any opportunity.

About this time Bill and I split up, we had a disagreement over a woman, so he went to the Columbia River, and I came here to Williams Creek.

I prospected this canyon, or gulch, and discovered that when the glaciers came down, eons ago, it changed the bed of Williams Creek, and covered over a large deposit of gold where it used to be. So I staked the ground, and by using scrapers, my hired help and I took off the sixteen feet of overburden, and then we mined it. The ground paid $1000 a foot, and I got very rich.

Of course when a fella gets rich, everybody wants to borrow money, but they never pay you back! I will be back next year to mine some more."

On returning to the newspaper office Dan worked up his notes on Neahmiah Smith, and submitted them to the editor.

"This is an excellent interview, Dan, now all I need are two others, Harry Jones, and Richard Willoughby."

"But first I want you to make a trip on horseback, immediately, to Van Winkle, where Mr. Jones lives in a camp on Chisholm Creek.

Starting out the very next morning, Dan went to Mundorfs' stables to pick up a horse.

"Better make sure his shoes are all in good shape, Mr Mundorf" said Dan, "I recently had an experience with a lost shoe that delayed my journey, and indeed, caused me a lot of trouble."

"I assure you" replied Joseph Mundorf, "I have personally checked this horse's feet and shoes. I guarantee you will have no trouble."

Fastening his bed roll and a sack of sandwiches on to the horse's back, Dan set off up the hill, past Richfield and up on to Bald Mountain.

From the many frozen patches of snow along the trail, it was evident that winter was very close upon them.

Out on the bare mountain Dan couldn't help looking over at the old cabin where he had sought refuge that day, and where he had first found the body of Richard Evans. 'What a terrible experience! How could anyone have done such a deed! Even now he could feel his stomach turn over at the very thought of it. It might not have been so bad if he had not been acquainted with the man before he was murdered.'

Still further on he passed Eagle Creek, where his horse's shoe was replaced. He wished that he had time to call on Mr Houseman again.

At Van Winkle he stopped at the hotel, where he enquired as to the whereabouts of the miner, Harry Jones.

Standing behind the desk in the lobby was the owner, Norman McCaffrey.

"I am surprised to see you still here", said Dan, "You told me you were leaving."

"No I didn't", he replied, "I told you I would not operate the post office any longer, because I was not being paid."

"Oh, you are quite right" agreed Dan, "now, can you tell me where I might find Harry Jones?"

"Harry Jones is mining on Peters Creek, about five or six miles from here. He and his partners operate the "Point Claim" there. We hear it is very rich."

"Is there a shortcut I can take from here, without having to retrace my steps?" asked Dan.

"Yes, you can ride up Chisholm Gulch, as far as Oregon Gulch, and then turn west to Peters Creek."

"Thanks for the information Sir, I have to find Jones, to get an interview." explained Dan.

"A what, did you say?" asked McCaffrey.

An interview, you know, for the newspaper!

"Oh yes" sighed McCaffrey.

Mr. McCaffrey offered Dan a beer before he left,

but of course Dan would not accept it.

"Do you mind if I sit and eat my lunch here?" he asked. "I would drink a Sarsaparilla if you have some."

"Certainly" replied McCaffrey, "how is everything at Williams Creek these days? Have they found the missing mine manager yet?"

"No" said Dan, remembering that he had promised not to divulge anything about it. Instead, he changed the subject.

"Most of the miners are about to leave for the winter." he continued. "Things around town are getting very quiet."

"Yes, they are here, also. My family and I are leaving next week for a trip to the States, to visit my wife's relatives."

By this time Dan was ready to leave, and thanking Mr McCaffrey for his hospitality, he got back on his horse again.

Traveling down Lightning Creek Dan came across several groups of miners still working their claims.

"The heavy frost is damaging our wooden pumps" they complained. "We will soon have to pack it up for the season."

As Dan reached Chisholm Gulch he came across several other mining camps, where it was obvious the miners were preparing to leave for the winter.

Turning down Oregon Gulch, Dan passed by several empty cabins, and silenced water wheels, where all was still save for several squirrels darting around,

204

preparing their last minute food caches for winter.

Several miles further on, and as the horse turned a corner on the trail, it began to behave strangely, shying to one side, and refusing to go forward. Dan looked around, and there on the edge of the timber ahead of them, was a pair of very large Siberian wolves. Occupied with eating a deer carcass, when they saw Dan and the horse, they snarled and sprang forward, showing their long, sharp teeth, in a very aggressive manner.

At this the horse got very nervous, rising up on its hind legs, and at one point Dan thought he was going to fall off. Finally he managed to settle the horse down, and steered it away from the wolves, taking a detour through the woods, to one side of the main trail..

'That was a close one' he thought, 'you never know what you are going to come across out here in the wilderness.'

Back on the trail again, Dan dismounted, and rested for a few minutes beside a fast flowing creek. While the horse drank from the creek, and grazed on the thin grass, he began to hear the distant sounds of a water wheel, creaking and groaning as it turned. As he continued to listen, he could also hear the sound of several voices, coming from somewhere not too far away.

'This must be Peters Creek' Dan told himself, 'I must be getting close to the 'Point' claim.'

Mounting the horse again, he rode on for another mile, and came upon a large mining operation, with several men moving around.

On the site was an enormous Cornish water wheel,

with a long flume made of lumber on one end.

Riding up to the doorway of one of several log cabins Dan dismounted, and tied the horse to a nearby hitching post.

"Hello," he called to a man standing there, "Is this the 'Point' claim? I am looking for Harry Jones, is he here?"

"Yes, he is the one over by the water wheel." answered the man.

Dan looked across the clearing, and saw a man attending to the water wheel. He was not a tall man, but had a sturdy build.

Finding his way through the piles of lumber and gravel, Dan reached the man and held out his hand.

"Good afternoon, Sir" he began, "I understand you are Harry Jones."

"Why yes," replied Harry, "and who are you?"

Dan explained who he was, and what he had been sent to do.

"We are very busy tidying up," said Jones, "getting ready to close the mine in a day or two. However, I know you have come a long way to see me, and I will not disappoint you. Let's go into the cook shack where we can talk, and have a cup of coffee." Jones suggested.

Leading the way, Harry took Dan over to a small log cabin behind the creek.

Inside, a cook stove almost as large as the cabin itself, took up most of the space, save for a large, rough table and several stools, where the men sat while they ate. The heat from the stove made it very warm, and as they entered, Harry kicked the door open.

"You are a Welshman" said Dan, "I can tell from your accent."

"Yes" said Harry, there are quite a few of us in the gold fields. You see that's because Welshmen are experienced in working in the tin mines in Wales, so we know a lot about cribbing and lagging for underground work."

"That's interesting", said Dan, "no one has explained that to me before. When did you come to the gold fields?"

"Originally I sailed from the old country in 1862, as one of Captain John Evans crew of twenty six Welsh Adventurers.

It took us two and a half months to reach the Cariboo, walking all the way from Victoria to the Captain's claim on Lightning Creek.

At first we had great faith in the Captain, for he was, as he told us, a mining engineer. We all worked hard, building cabins, the water wheel, and other structures on the claim, but when it came to mining, there was hardly a flake of gold to be found."

As Harry made a pot of coffee, and laid out two cups, he continued on, "Miners on the opposite bank of Lightning Creek were finding lots of gold, but there was none on the Captain's claim. For two years we worked, and toward the end, when the money from the sponsor in England stopped coming, we were almost starved for food, and some of us got scurvy, from a lack of vegetables.

Finally, a few of our members decided they had had enough, and walked off. Before long, most of the twenty six men had left.

Captain Evan's son, Taliesin, and I were the last to leave. From then on we were on our own in a strange land, and unable to speak much English."

"That must have been very difficult for you" said Dan, "but you would have learned English quickly, out of necessity, I expect."

"Yes", agreed Harry, "but I have never learned to write English properly."

"But it hasn't stopped you from making a living!" put in Dan.

"No" Harry went on, "it took a long time, but now I do manage to make myself understood. Perhaps this has made me sympathetic toward the Chinese miners. There is great prejudice against them, and I think it is because they are misunderstood."

"Perhaps so" agreed Dan, "I have some Chinese friends that live at Cottonwood, and I have found them to be very honest and straight forward."

"I was actually able to help the members of one Chinese mining company last year, when some Europeans tried to cheat them out of their claims" mentioned Harry.

"Were you successful?" Dan asked.

"Yes, with my help, the Chinese were able to prove that the Europeans were dishonest, and they lost their mining licenses."

"Served them right!" said Dan, "have you been back to Wales since you came out to Canada?" asked Dan

"As a matter of a fact, I am sailing for home this winter. This mining claim we call 'the Point', has been very rich, so much so that I will be able to take some time off to visit my mother, and other relatives."

By now the other men were coming into the cabin. "Time to cook supper, Harry," said one.

"It is getting too late for you to get back to Williams Creek tonight, Dan, you had better plan on staying the night." suggested Harry.

"I agree", said Dan, "I will look after my horse, and fetch my pack."

"You can turn your horse out in that little corral over yonder, he will be safe there for the night." said Harry as he and Dan left the cabin.

Dan was up early the next morning, and after a bit of breakfast and a cup of hot coffee, he left Harry Jones and the 'Point' claim, and headed back toward Lightning Creek

CHAPTER 12

Of Ghouls and Gold Strikes.

By noon the weather had turned a bit nasty, with dark clouds in the sky, and a cold wind blowing from the north.

'Looks like snow coming' Dan said to himself.'

'I hope I can get back in time to find Richard Willoughby at the Lowhee mine for an interview. Then I will have these interviews all done.'

By the time Dan reached Van Winkle Creek, a blizzard had started, but he managed to get the horse watered and put in to a barn, before he ran into the hotel.

"Well Dan, you couldn't have arrived at a more opportune moment." said Mr. McCaffrey in a state of great excitement. "There has been a big gold strike on Lightning Creek, made by the Costello company of miners. This is going to give Van Winkle, and in fact the whole community a real economic boost," Norman McCaffrey went on. "Perhaps you could write a newspaper article about it."

McCaffrey was so excited about the gold strike that he kept following Dan around and telling him more.

"The Costello Company have been trying for months to get down to bedrock, and today they made a fantastic strike. They say it was only possible due to the use of the new, metal pumps they recently acquired.

210

The old wooden pumps were always breaking down."

"I suppose the men of the Costello Company are down at their mine, are they? inquired Dan.

"Yes, they are." said McCaffrey. "If you go down there, ask for John Costello, he is the leader of the group. If I'm not mistaken, he's a brother to James Costello who was with Bill Dietz and his associates on Williams Creek in 1860."

After a bite of lunch Dan rode his horse down Lightning Creek for about a mile and a half, past several groups of miners at work in the creek. Inspite of the wintry weather, there seemed to be a hightened enthusiasm amongst the miners, due in part to the success of the Costello Company.

"We have invested in metal pumps too" they told Dan, who was getting their comments on the strike." So hopefully we will also get down to the gold." they said excitedly.

The activity around the Costello mine, and the adjoining claims of the Vulcan, Lightning, and Clarke companies was like a hive of bees making a swarm. Even the imminent arrival of winter did not deter them. Actually the heavy frost in the ground had thickened the slum which was so prevalent in Lightning Creek, making it easier to control.

Down at the Costello mine Dan tried, but found it impossible to talk to the mine owners. They were all too busy, and too excited over the strike. Having gained sufficient information about the strike from McCaffrey, and a few of the other miners, Dan left Van Winkle, and headed back to Williams Creek.

It was late in the evening when he reached the town, his horse having ploughed through several inches of snow over Bald Mountain.

Despite the late hour, George Wallace was still at the Sentinel office and gave Dan a warm welcome back.

"I must congratulate you on your efforts, Dan, you are shaping up to be a first class reporter. The news about the strike on Lightning Creek will make a very exciting article in the next paper, although I wonder how many will still be here to read it."

Dan had to leave just then, to take the horse back to the stables.

"I will be back in a few minutes" he told George. Before he left though, George asked him:

"Do you think you could still get an interview from Richard Willoughby?"

"If he has not left yet, to go south." replied Dan.

As Dan lead the horse up to Mundorf's stables, he passed by Kwai Chung's 'Laundry and Hot Baths' shop.

'I wonder how Ah Fat's funeral went' he thought, 'I must contact John Boyd to see how the negotiations are going, to bring his daughter over from China.'

Early the next morning, before going to work, Dan climbed the hill to Richfield to see Collette.

'She has been rather depressed lately' he thought, 'what with her mother whining about money, and she herself wondering where to find another job.'

212

Collette was not out of bed when Dan reached the house, so he peered through the windows until he decided which was her bedroom.

Tapping on the glass a few times, it roused Collette, and she came to the window.

"I got back last night from Peters and Lightning Creek, I have a lot of news to tell you. Would you have breakfast with me, at the "Wake-Up-Jake?" he asked.

"I will get dressed, and meet you at the front door" replied Collette.

It was very quiet in the restaurant, so Dan and Collette were able to have a lengthy visit.

"I have been thinking about our futures, Collette." Dan began, "At one point I would have asked you to marry me, but you are so young, and have a brilliant future ahead of you as a dancer. Although I love you dearly, I feel I have no right to deprive you of the chance. If we were married, it would change all that."

"Yes Dan," said Collette, taking his hand "You also have many talents, and should be allowed to discover them before you become encumbered with a wife."

Perhaps our lives will find each other again at a later time" suggested Dan.

As Dan looked over at Collette, he could see that she was crying.

"I am so sorry to have made you cry, my dear, I am sure better times will come soon."

At this point Dan thought that if he changed the subject, it might relieve the tension.

"I have just one more interview to do, before I am

finished." he told her, "so it may be a few more days before we can go together to see Beavan Jones about Owen Parry.

"I hope you find Richard Willoughby, I have heard that he doesn't stay in one place for very long." Collette mentioned as she wiped her eyes..

The next day Dan took a horse with him to climb the steep hill up to the Lowhee mine. On the way he passed by Ned Stout's mine, and the abandoned workings of the Welsh Company. From some distance he noticed Mrs. Evans out in her garden, preparing it for winter.

Having climbed to the top of the hill, Dan lead the horse down the slope on to the north side, and the site of the mine buildings, about half way from the valley below.

The several structures were large, built of lumber, with an enormous Cornish water wheel beside the creek. Having decided on which was the main building, Dan rode up to the door and knocked.

"Enter" said a loud voice, as Dan went in. He had picked the right building, it had to be the office, for the walls contained shelves stacked with books and papers, from the floor to the ceiling.

Seated behind a large mahogany desk covered with papers, left over pots of tea, and plates of half eaten sandwiches, sat a tall individual with a head of black, curly hair. He had a long stemmed pipe in his mouth, the smoke from which permeated the room, and caused Dan to cough a few times.

"Excuse me Sir", said Dan, "Are you Richard Willoughby? I am a reporter from the Sentinel newspaper, on Williams Creek, and I am hoping you will give me an interview."

"Why would you want to interview me?" he asked.

"I believe you to be one of the pioneer miners in this region of the Cariboo." replied Dan, "and from what I hear, I am extremely fortunate to find you here."

"Yes, as a matter of a fact that is true, I am tidying up the company papers in preparation for my departure tomorrow."

"Can you spare a few minutes to talk to me, Sir? I want to know a bit about your background." said Dan, as he sat down on a wooden office chair.

"Well, get your pencil ready." said Willoughby.

"Although my parents were originally from England, I was born in Missouri. My father was a famous scout and Indian fighter, and by age sixteen I was off with him, sharing his adventures."

"You mean you left your mother, and went off with your father?"

"Yes, I had learned to play the violin at an early age, and my mother was heart broken when I refused an offer to follow a career in music. Not long after that I was with a band of Texas cowboys, and fought in the war against Mexico."

"In 1849 I mined successfully in the California gold rush, and later was leader of a wagon train of four hundred men and women who traveled across the

United States to Oregon.

By 1858 I had journeyed to the gold rush on the lower Fraser River. I fought the Indians with Captain Snyder, and after a three day war, a truce was called, and we were allowed to mine again on the river."

"Well, you must have come across Ned Stout; he had the same experiernce" interrupted Dan.

"Yes," said Willoughby, I have often reminisced over those times with Stout." he recalled.

"I did really well mining on Emmory Bar, not far north of Yale, and cleaned up $20,000 after only a few weeks work."

"Were you there at the same time as the Emmory brothers?" Dan asked.

"Yes, John, who died this year, was sick even then." As Dan looked over at Richard Willoughby, he saw a far away look in his eye, as if recalling some experience. After a few moments he recovered, and continued,

"Then I made the mistake of my life by investing in several other adjoining claims on Emmory, and lost everything.

I arrived in the Cariboo broke and discouraged.

Prospecting around at Keithley and Burns Creek, I mined a few ounces, and got a grubstake from the storekeeper on Burns Creek. Within a few weeks I had discovered and staked several claims on what I named the 'Great Lowhee Mine'. I never looked back."

"What was the 'Lowhee', Sir?" asked Dan.

"It was a secret miner's protective society that I belonged to, in the lower Fraser." replied Willoughby.

"You are full of information, Sir, no wonder my editor demanded that I interview you" said Dan, whose notebook was crammed full, and his pencil almost worn out.

"Where are you going to for the winter, Sir?"

"To San Francisco, young man, where I have other business to attend to."

"I want to thank you for your patience with me." mentioned Dan as he left Richard Willoughby and rode back to Williams Creek.

It was a few days later, on a bright and sunny morning, when Dan took some time off to be with Collette.

Today they would go together to talk with Beavan Jones, concerning Owen Parry.

The police had already confirmed that Owen, like Richard Evans, had not left Williams Creek, and that they definitely suspected foul play.

Mrs. Evans had been told that her husband's murdered body had been found, but that it had also disappeared again. In her unhappy state she had sent for her sister who lived in California, to be with her.

"I must have Richard's body back for burial" she had sobbed to Constable Fitzgerald, "I can't stand the idea that someone is moving his body around like this."

Up at the deserted Welsh Co. mine, a cold wind howled around the shaft house, while a loose piece of metal on the Cornish Wheel rattled with every gust.

Dan and Collette looked for Beavan in the mine office, but no one was there. With the mine shut down, and all the men dismissed, it was like an empty tomb.

"What a desolate place it can be" mentioned Collette as she fastened her coat collar a little tighter.

"Let's go up to Beavan's cabin," suggested Dan, "we will probably find him there."

As they trudged up the hill, they noticed the many footprints, and tracks of horses and sleighs, in the snow, going to and fro from the various residences

On reaching Beavan Jones cabin, Dan knocked on the front door. It was opened almost immediately, by Beavan, who invited them in.

As a confirmed batchelor, Beavan Jones was indeed a most tidy person. His one room cabin had been completely organized into a bedroom, kitchen, and sitting room apartment.

As he walked over to the big iron cook stove to put the kettle on to boil, he mentioned:

"I understand you and Owen were to be married soon, Collette?"

Yes," she replied, "but now I am I am not so sure."

Collette was unable to complete her sentence, when Beavan interrupted.

"If you will ever see him again? Do you know that Owen is a thief? I can prove it from my accounts, that he must have stolen quite a few pounds of gold from the mine."

"Can you prove that it was Owen who took the gold?" asked Dan, as Beavan. handed him a cup of tea

218

"No one else would have access to it" said Beavan, his Welsh accent sending his voice up an octave, "I think Owen has 'flown the coop' so to speak, with the gold."

"The last time I spoke with him," added Collette, "he was anxious to get married, and go off on a honeymoon, but I managed to put him off."

"Well, apparently he did not wait for you" put in Beavan.

"Since then the police have confirmed that Owen has not left the creek by any conventional means." divulged Collette.

"Humph" said Beavan, "it sounds a lot like Richard Evan's disappearance."

"Yes, it does", said Dan, who was having a very hard time to keep from telling Beavan what he knew.

"Why do you suppose Richard disappeared?" asked Dan.

"I cannot answer that question" said Beavan, "it has to do with company policy."

"So you have no idea where Owen Parry is?" asked Collette.

"I suspect that he has gone off with the gold he stole from the mine, but as yet I have no proof."

Dan would have agreed with Beavan, that Owen Parry was a slippery charecter. The example of his missing gold coin was proof enough, but he could not mention any of this to Beavan.

Having exhausted their discussion concerning Owen Parry, Dan and Collette left Beavan Jones, and started off down the mountain. They had gone just a few feet, when Collette stopped.

"Let's have a longer walk, Dan, it's such a lovely day. We could go by way of Lowhee Creek, and back by way of Williams Creek, if you would agree."

"Well, alright, but that's a very long walk. Are you sure you are up to it? Perhaps we could find a shorter trail that would take us back to Williams Creek."

"I love exploring" said Collette, who was quite taken with the bright, clear day. In her exuberance she was performing pirouettes up on her toes.

"You are such a butterfly" said Dan as he took Collette into his arms and kissed her soundly.

"And you are such a charming escort" she said as she danced off along the upward trail.

They walked through several inches of fresh snow, along a narrow path and up over the crest of the mountain. Here and there were huge piles of mine tailings. Covered with clean, white snow, they resembled icebergs.

"Oh look Dan, there's a tunnel. I dare you to go in there. Perhaps you can see gold in the veins on the walls!" shouted Collette from a distance.

"Don't be ridiculous, come back" Dan called back, "it's dangerous to wander into a tunnel without at least a lantern."

Before Dan could stop her, Collette had entered the tunnel, with Dan after her.

"Come back, you silly girl" he called from the entrance, but there was no answer.

"Collette," Dan called several times, but still there was no answer.

As he had told Collette, it was dangerous to enter a tunnel without at least a lantern. 'What could have happened to Collette?' he wondered. Dan blamed himself for letting her go in, but he had tried to stop her!

Without a lantern it was hopeless to search for Collette. Turning back on the trail, Dan ran almost all the way back to Beavan's cabin, and rapped anxiously on the door. As he stood there trying to catch his breath, there was no answer to his knocks, Beavan was gone.

Then Dan went into Beavan's shed beside the cabin, and there he found a coal oil lantern, which fortunately had some oil in it.

'Now I need some matches, or a flint' he told himself. Searching around on the neatly arranged shelves Dan found a metal box of 'Bell & Black's' wax matches, which he put into his pocket. There were three matches left in the box.

Running back up the trail he couldn't help noticing an extra set of boot tracks in the snow, tracks that he had not seen before.

Reaching the mouth of the tunnel, Dan called again, and this time he could hear Collette's voice answering.

"Dan," she called in a hoarse whisper, I have fallen into a test hole; I fell a long way, and knocked myself out. It is wet down here. Can you get me out? You will need a strong rope." Then she added, "I think there is more than just me down here."

"What do you mean 'more than just me down

here?' asked Dan.

"I think there are some dead bodies down here. I can't really see, it's so dark here, but there's a terrible smell."

Dan lit the lantern and crept along the wall of the tunnel, until he came to a wooden structure built over a wide test hole.

"Collette?" he called. "are you down there?"

"Yes" replied Collette, "I think I have twisted my ankle."

'Oh rats, I should have thought of bringing a rope' he told himself.

Just then, as Dan turned toward the entrance of the tunnel, he caught sight of someone standing out in the bright sunlight.

"Hey you there," he called, "can you help me, my friend has fallen down a hole."

As Dan hurried toward the light, he saw the figure, but when he reached the entrance, no one was there.

With that Dan ran back to the shaft and called:

"Collette, can you hear me?"

"Yes," she called back, sounding as if she was crying.

"I am going to go and get help, and a rope. Please try to hold on, and be sure, I am going to get you out of there." called Dan.

"Please hurry" Collette called back, "I am in great pain and it's cold, and very smelly down here."

With that Dan hurried out of the tunnel, and stopped again at Beavan Jones cabin, but still there was no one there. Out in the shed Dan found a long, stout rope, which he coiled up and threw over his shoulder, as he hurried on to the next cabin. There he found Bill Griffiths, an employee of the Welsh Co. mine. Bill was a strong young man, a good candidate to help Dan.

"Can you come and help me? Collette Dumais has fallen down a test hole in a tunnel on Lowhee Mountain. I found a good rope, and if you will come with me to make sure we get out alive, I will go down the hole to rescue the lady."

"Yes, of course" he replied "lets go."

On nearing the tunnel, Dan was sure he saw someone walking near the entrance, but once again, when they got there, the person had gone.

As they reached the hole, they could hear someone singing. It was Collette, she was singing the French national anthem, "La Marseillaise" to keep herself occupied while she waited to be rescued.

"Collette" Dan called, "I am back, and I have Bill Griffiths with me. I also have a strong rope. Hold on while I come down."

"Bring a lantern with you, so we can see what else is down here" called Collette.

While Bill Griffiths tied one end of the rope securely to the wooden scaffolding above the hole, Dan tied himself to the other, and holding the lighted lantern in one hand, he slowly let him self down. Balancing his feet on the solid rock sides of the hole, he bounced from rock to rock until he was down at the bottom, about twenty feet from the surface. The further down he went, the more putrid was the smell.

Curled up on the driest side of the hole was Collette, whose sprained ankle prevented her from going to Dan, but he quickly found her, and embraced her warmly.

"Oh Collette, my dear" he murmered as he held her, "I am so glad you are not hurt too badly."

Shining the lantern over to the other side of the hole, Dan could see two dead bodies, lying face down, one on top of the other. Turning them over, he identified Richard Evans, and Owen Parry. They had both been stabbed in the back.

"We will wait for the police before we move them, but for now we will concentrate on getting you out" he said as he made a rope seat, and fastened Collette in to it.."

"You know a lot about working with ropes, don't you Dan" exclaimed Collette.

"I worked with ropes while out fishing with my father." replied Dan.

Calling to Bill Griffiths to start pulling on the rope, Dan warned Collette to keep off the rough rocks on the sides, as she went up.

Just as Collette was about half way up, the rope went slack, and she came down again with a great thump. Luckily Dan caught her before she reached the bottom, and they fell together in a heap.

"What is the problem, Bill, is it too much for you?" called Dan. Just then Dan and Collette heard a great scuffle going on up above.

As Bill was pulling hard on the rope, Beavan Jones entered the tunnel and attacked him.

It must have been Beavan Jones that Dan had seen lurking around the entrance to the tunnel! "I'm going to put you down there with Dan and Collette, and the other two" he said between gasps, as he fought with Bill.

"I don't think so" replied Bill, and with one great punch Bill sent Beavan careening over the edge, and down into the hole.

Having got rid of Beavan, Bill Griffiths ran out of the tunnel, and went to get help.

Beavan was still conscious when he landed at the bottom of the hole, and with a shake of his head, he got up and tackled Dan.

Collette had managed to move over to the other side of the pit. Walking around the dead bodies, she crouched down in terror, watching Dan as he fought with Beavan.

"You and your inquisitive reporting", he said to Dan, "I had Richard safely put away, when you had to discover him at that old cabin."

"It was purely by accident, that I happened to be there." shouted Dan as he avoided Beavan's blows.

"Why did you kill your mining partners Beavan?" asked Dan as he ran over to the other side of the pit.

"I was embezzling the gold, and they were about to expose me." he answered as he tackled Dan.

By this time Collette had collected herself, and saw that Beavan was about to overcome Dan. Noticing a large rock that lay close to her, she picked it up, and when Beavan wasn't looking, she hit him hard on the head.

He was out like a light, and lay stretched out beside his dead partners.

In spite of her lame ankle, Collette went over to Dan, and hugged him.

"That was fast thinking on your part, Collette" he said "I was just about all in when you hit him."

As they stood holding eachother, they could hear voices coming from the surface of the hole.

Bill was back, and with him, Sergeant Fitzgerald and his deputy.

"Hold on there" the Sergeant called down the hole, "while we get this rope going again. First, I want you to send up Beavan Jones. He is going to have to answer to his despicable crimes, but first he will be held in jail until next spring when Judge Begbie arrives to hold court."

Beavan was barely conscious as Dan and Collette tied the rope securely around his waist and under his arms, before he was pulled up.

Then it was Collette's turn, and after that Dan, who told the story of finding the two bodies down in the pit.

"Well actually," he admitted, "if Collette had not fallen into the hole, we may never have found them."

Picking up a large rock, Collette struck Beavan hard, on the head.

News of the recovery of two bodies from a test hole on Lowhee mountain shook the community of Williams Creek, in fact the whole of Cariboo, for quite some time.

The headline article on the front page of the *Sentinel* newspaper described how Collette had fallen down the hole, and found herself sharing it with two decomposing bodies.

Mine manager Beavan Jones, of the Welsh Co. mine on Caenarvon Mountain, had been arrested and charged with the murders of his two partners, Richard Evans and Owen Parry.

With a lack of advertising sponsors for the winter season, George Wallace, owner of the *Sentinel* newspaper, decided to discontinue the publishing of the paper until the next spring.

Now that Collette's fiance Owen Parry was deceased, Collette's mother was beside herself with worry as to how she and Collette would survive the winter.

Dan, while his job with the newspaper had ceased for the winter, was recommended by Sergeant Fitzgerald for a job as a detective. This meant that he would have to leave Williams Creek to take a police training course in Winnipeg.

"Oh, and by the way, Dan, you can have your gold coin back now" Sergeant Fitzgerald told him, "Beavan must have taken it from Owen Parry when he killed him."

A few days later, just as Dan and George Wallace were preparing to leave Williams Creek on the stage,

Collette and her mother arrived at the Sentinel office.

"Dan, she announced, "We have come to see you off, but first I have some very good news. Madame Bendixon has offered to sponsor me for some ballet lessons in a well established school in Paris." Mrs. Dumais was also delighted, for now she could get back to her familiar lifestyle in France.

"Well", said George Wallace to Dan as he closed the office of the *Cariboo Sentinel,* and picked up his bags, "I wonder what mischief we can dig up for the paper next year!"

The End.

ISBN 141203664-X